PRAISE FOR SHANGHAIED

"Jon Howe has created a narrative that is at once gripping and eminently human. With a keen eye for the time and place of his tale, Howe weaves a tale of resilience and the longing to reclaim what's been lost. Eamon McGrath takes his place alongside Melville's Ishmael and Jack London's Humphrey Van Weyden as characters whom the sea and its sailors would claim, but who remain true to their innate humanity. Well and often lyrical, this is a remarkable debut novel."

—Greg Fields, Author of *Through the Waters and the Wild*, 2022 Winner, Independent Press Award for Literary Fiction

"In a moment, I found myself on board, high in the creaking rigging of a square rigger, deep in the restlessness of the high seas, awash in the well-written words of Jon Howe's first novel. He's done his research on time and place in a seaworthy story of survival."

—Jim Lawrence, Author of *Callused Hands, Hungry Heart*

Shanghaied

by Jon Tritschler Howe

© Copyright 2023 Jon Tritschler Howe

ISBN 979-8-88824-126-4

Published by

 köehlerbooks™

3705 Shore Drive
Virginia Beach, VA 23455
800-435-4811
www.koehlerbooks.com

SHANGHAIED

JON HOWE

VIRGINIA BEACH
CAPE CHARLES

Table of Contents

"... I want to know
if you are prepared to live in this world
with its harsh need
to change you ..."

SELF-PORTRAIT by David Whyte

CHAPTER 1

A **SHOCK OF** cold water wakes Eamon.

He is in too much pain to care what brings him up from the dark. His whole body feels bruised, numb, and twisted. His spine and limbs are getting painful revenge for whatever way he crumpled, unconscious. As he tries to orient, these first few seconds feel slow but dizzily accelerate. Before his questions cascade, before he pries his eyes open, something in his gut is heavy beyond all experience. It informs him with terrible certainty that something is wrong, unbelievably wrong, that it will crash in on him, that there is nothing he can do about it. Where does this information come from? How could his senses learn anything while he lay near dead?

His first thought takes shape around a stench, but impressions are not yet words. Next are sounds, something creaking and water. *Surf?* His cheek is wet, pressed against a wooden floor. He feels motion. Sudden and wide, he opens his eyes. The first thing he sees is the sole of a shoe close by his face. His arms push him up of their own quick volition. "Aach!" He is surrounded by semi-darkness. Attached to that shoe is a person, inert on the floor. And another next to him, and another. Now his thoughts race. *Who are they? What are we doing on the pub floor?* He tries to fit what is happening into his memory of last night: the warmth at The King's Rook, the crowd singing worse and louder as they drink more. *Wait.* The floor is indeed moving. *This isn't the pub floor!* He tries to rise, but halfway up loses balance, reaches out, finds nothing to grab onto, and tumbles to an awkward sitting position, almost landing on another body. There are four of them.

Looking for anything familiar, rubbing panicked eyes, his first words slur weakly out, "Where-m I?" His voice sounds distant to himself. "Wha's happening?" To clear his mind, he shakes his head. It hurts. He rubs the back of it. He catches sight of a figure distant in the shadows: a man standing carelessly steady, one hand raised to the low ceiling to steady himself and a wooden bucket in the other. Eamon frowns. "Who're *you*? Where the hell am I?" The rage in his voice contrasts with fear and weakness in his heart.

Behind the man, there is a ladder in a glaring patch of sunlight. His tall silhouette is thin, and he stoops to duck the overhead. He has a mop of hair and a beard, a loose shirt, and ragged breeches tied with a cord. His feet are bare. Uncaring, he replies with a voice as casual as his stance, "Welcome aboard, mate." He turns to walk toward the ladder but looks back when he hears the emotion in Eamon's voice.

"Becca! Oh no! And Alex and Amy. Lord, no!"

The intensity the man hears surpasses him. He climbs the ladder, vanishing into the light.

"I'm on a ship!" Eamon almost gags on his words. "Bloody hell! This can't be! I've got to get off." Attacked by each approaching second, he shakes his head and squeezes his eyes shut, only to open them again to this nightmare. He cannot fight the seconds off. *If we're within sight of land . . . but it's too cold to swim. Maybe I can bribe the captain to go back. Or I'll lie that he's got the wrong man, that I'm important and he's in trouble.*

At a loss, he glances about and struggles to his feet. *I'll take a boat on deck, even if I have to fight for it. I can tell east from west.* Weaving toward the ladder, grimacing, he stops and turns back. *But I can't do it alone. Maybe I can recruit the others.*

They are coming to, rubbing their heads and necks. Their pains echo Eamon's own. He comes back the few unsteady steps and lowers himself to one knee to help the biggest of them sit up. "We've been kidnapped, stolen! We're on a ship. And the sooner we get off, the better chance we have to get back. Can you get to your feet? We might have to fight our way out of here."

"Slow down, will ya?" The man looks about. "By God, you're serious!" He turns to Eamon. "Aren't you the printer?"

"Yes, I'm serious. And I'm Eamon. You're Sam, right?"

"Right. Wouldn't think you knew my name as little as you go out. Looks like you picked the wrong night, though. Must've been somethin' in the beer." The glaze over Sam's eyes is clearing. "Y'know, I've got crops to get in."

"You'll not be getting crops in from the middle of the ocean."

A groggy younger voice asks from behind Eamon, "Wud he say, Sam?"

"Coop! You're here too? Mercy."

Eamon goes to help the young man. "The middle of the ocean, that's what I said. We'll be there if we don't get busy. We've been kidnapped. You're on a ship, and the longer you take to get off, the farther you'll have to row to go back."

"You're crazy!" The young man leans away from Eamon. As the ship rolls, he plants his hands on the deck as if to hold it still. His eyes widen. "Whoa! Maybe you're not."

"Heed me; we've got to muster up here. If we fight for one of the boats on deck, we might have a chance."

"Yer right, lad. He's crazy," a deep voice starts. The oldest of the victims sits with his back against what they now know to be the hull of a ship. He massages his neck while he rolls his head back and forth. "It's called shanghaied. We've been shanghaied. They've thrown us in an empty hold, taken us to sea, and don't need to lock us up. There's nowhere to run out here. And if I've ever heard of gettin' home after this, I haven't believed it."

Coop worries. "If we fight the captain and crew, wouldn't it be mutiny? They hang people for that!"

"Mutiny? You cannot be serious!" Eamon almost shouts. "To kidnap someone is a crime. We can't be hung for doing what it takes to go back. I don't care what they call it. I have GOT to get home.

And I can't do it alone, but between the five of us, we might be able to hold them off."

"Between the four of us," Sam interrupts. "This one's dead." They all wince. Sam has crawled to where he can reach the cold neck of the body wearing the shoe Eamon first saw. "You can see what our lives are worth, eh? Back home, this is murder, but out here, he'll get tossed over the side, and no one will know."

"Do ya see now?" the older man agrees. "We best be tryin' to survive instead of tryin' to get home. Our homes is here now."

"Who?" Coop looks askance at the dead man. "Who is he?"

"Does it matter? He's dead. He's nobody now."

"But someone should be told," Coop almost whispers.

"There's no one to tell. None of us was a motherless child, but we all are now. The sooner ya get over it, the better. Yer part of a crew, and it's yer next breath ya better worry about. What good are ya if yer dead?"

Eamon jolts from staring at the body. "It's the same bloody thing. Our home can't be here. We've got families and crops and trades. We can't just vanish from our lives. Look, we don't have time to argue. Are you with me or not?"

"Have mercy, but I'm not with ya. I've been here before. Wish I could say it weren't so, but 'tis. My skipper won't be happy I don't come back, but he'll figure it out. He'll pocket my wages and replace me easy enough."

"You're one of them? A sailor?" Coop asks.

"Aye, for more than thirty year now. I stopped countin'. I wasn't shanghaied, though. I ran away. My family was starvin' and didn't need another mouth to feed. I was young and full of pluck. Shanghaiin' started aboard men of war, but when merchant ships lost crew to the navies, they learned it too. My blood, I should'a seen it comin' when that crew come in the pub last night. I've followed those orders myself."

"What? You've kidnapped men?" Eamon wants to strike the man, but they both know his anger is useless. "You . . . blackheart!"

"Ya don't know what you're in for. You'll learn to follow orders. Sometimes it's the only way to fight for yer life."

"But this is not my life! My life is back there. There's nothing here to fight for." Eamon starts feeling dizzy.

"Then you'll be out'a yer misery soon enough and swimmin' with our dead friend. Ya better hope this ship's desperate for crew so ya live long enough to get down off yer horse."

Eamon breaks into a sweat. He drops to his knees, braces a hand against the hull, and vomits a barely discreet distance from the man. Sam is soon doing the same.

"Yer too seasick to fight anyway, yer lordship."

Between heaves, Eamon scowls sideways at him.

Coop suggests they need fresh air, so they help each other to their feet.

"Don't be tryin' anythin' fancy up there, mates," the man bids them. "Just get to the rail and get yer bearings. Any ship that shanghais is rough enough. We're sure in for a long trip without makin' it worse."

As they start for the ladder, Sam stops them. "Y'know, maybe we should know your name if we're mates. I'm Sam. I'm a farmer. This here is Coop, the cooper's son. And that's Eamon, the printer."

"I'm Jack, bosun's mate on . . . on my last ship. And we're all sailors now, so let's stick together. With a little luck, I'll get ya through another day."

Leaning on each other, they stagger toward the ladder. There they are blinded by sunlight. Add to that their lack of sea legs; it is no wonder that when they stumble up on deck, the only one left standing is Jack. He tries to help them up and glances over his shoulder at the same time.

CHAPTER 2

EAMON IS FRANTIC to scan the horizon. He doesn't wait for Jack's help. Oblivious to the ship's landscape and crew, he half-crawls, half-runs for the portside, up the deck's slant, away from the water racing by to starboard. When Jack catches sight of their "welcoming committee," Eamon is beyond his reach. He asks Sam for Eamon's name, to call him back, but forces are in motion. If this goes badly, he hopes there will be pieces left to pick up.

Unaware of the sight he is and the sounds he makes, Eamon's entire focus is on the nearest object, heedless whether it's made of wood, cloth, hemp, or flesh. As long as it serves as a handhold or foothold, he scrambles toward the rail, not noticing the derision he draws.

When he gets to the gunwale, he squints into a blast of wind and spray. The scene before him is riotous. Under a cold sun, waves crash to an empty horizon. It strikes him like a blow, shattering his hope of getting off the ship. The shards of those hopes slice something inside him. He feels himself bleeding from mortal wounds that no one can see, and there is no defense.

"NOOOO!!" howls out of him. He squeezes his eyes shut. "Oh, Lord, no." He doesn't know what he sobs next. No breath can speak it. His jaw clenches, yet words spew out. "I can't be here. I'm . . . NO, GOD DAMN!"

What the crew witnesses takes them by surprise. They've never seen grief so manifest. This madman arrives on deck spattered in puke and moving like a monkey. Despite stumbling, he is strong and fast. He runs right over the top of a crew member sitting with his back against a hatch. At the rail, when Eamon's body curls in pain, they all suspect the man he ran over, but he holds no weapon and gestures innocence. Eamon winces and contorts as if a ghost is stabbing him. His hands flail to ward off an invisible attacker. His fingers curl and spread. When he buries his face in them, the men half expect it to emerge bloody. Their superstitions stirred, the sailors exchange nervous glances. He starts to slump to the deck but writhes back up, his head half thrown back, a random grip on the rigging, and another ragged sound tears from him. The crew recoils from his gaze; there is no safe distance from that look. In the next second, he sees through them as if they aren't there. *Why would the bosun shanghai a lunatic?*

At last, he collapses next to the bulwark, heaving dry. He pounds the deck weakly and mutters, "No. Oh no." Inside himself, Eamon indeed drops over an edge, goes mad. In the ship's lingo, he "cuts himself adrift."

The first mate sees this affecting his men, and he'll afford none of it. "You!" he shouts to the nearest sailor. "Get the bosun up here while I straighten this out." He has risen to his rank by brute force, and he will die before he loses command. This makes him different from the crew. This and the fact that he likes a fight. With the rush of adrenaline, his pulse becomes a drumbeat in his ears, and he feels more alive. This time, he is a third bigger than his victim, who can hardly even stand. *Short work this,* but he hopes not too short. He feels the crew's attention and intends to impress them. Starting toward the tormented man, he roars, "You there!"

Eamon is far gone, yet his instincts warn him of the mate's approach. Lacking sea legs, he grasps a piece of rigging to stand and turns to face the man. His senses begin to return. Smells, sounds, the wind on his neck—none of it coherent and all beyond caring, but details get through. The man coming toward him is more than imposing. He is tall and broad, his neck thick and limbs large. His beard hides half of a scar on his right cheek. His teeth are mottled. His black hair is tied back into a dirty tail with a red kerchief. Unlike the other men, he wears shoes. His white stockings reach above his knees to his breeches, also white. While most of the men on board secure their trousers with a length of rope, he wears a broad belt and buckle. A blue waistcoat covers his dull linen shirt.

Eamon loses the man's words but can see his intention. What has been pure pain in Eamon snaps into rage. When his right hand comes loose from the rail, it's with a belaying pin in hand. As if by magic, he holds a cudgel. With no idea what he is doing, he hurls himself at his attacker.

The mate is caught off guard. Usually, he goads his victims and corners them into a fight, but this man is insane. When they retell the story, the crew will say that Eamon was foaming at the mouth, snarling like an animal. The exaggeration will be only slight.

Eamon's rush gains momentum down the slant of the decks. He pushes off the raised edge of a hatch, kicks his feet toward the mate's torso, and swings the belaying pin like a club.

The mate turns so that Eamon's weight glances off and he dodges the blow easily. As his opponent flails by, out of control, he hasn't planned on Eamon's other hand trailing behind and latching into his hair. The mate's head snaps around with Eamon's full weight and momentum. "Bloody hell!" He finds himself sprawled on deck with this demon on his back, pulling his hair and clubbing him.

The crew has never seen the mate fall. They are quick to trade foregone conclusions for real interest. One blow lands hard on the side of the mate's head; his vision blurs with stars. *This won't do,* he thinks. Even with the smaller man on his back, he leaps to his feet and wards off the next blow. He needs to loosen this grip on his hair, get him around in front where he can do something to him.

The mate backs up fast. There is an audible crack when their combined weight strikes the mainmast. The crew half groans at the sound of the impact. Eamon gasps and tries to take back his breath while dodging the mate's blindly grasping hands. He hangs on like a man on a bucking horse while the mate spins around. The mate grabs the wrist of Eamon's hand that tugs at his hair and catches the other arm. He bends forward as fast and far as he can. Eamon loses hold of the pin but not the hair as he flips over the mate's head, landing on his back, his head toward the mate. The mate resists the pull on his scalp for a moment and then drives his head down to break Eamon's nose.

"YOU are a DEAD man!" he bellows.

Their faces inches apart, Eamon flinches away from his opponent's putrid breath. The mate's hands latch onto Eamon's face and pound his head onto the deck. A thumb digs into one eye socket. His vision blurs with pain. With both of his own hands, Eamon grasps the mate's wrist but can't pull away the hand that is about to blind him. He thrashes his head back and forth. When spit, blood, and snot make the mate's grip slip, Eamon feels a finger in his mouth. He bites down as hard as he can and hears the mate howl. His teeth almost pull out of his head. The mate smashes Eamon's face with his free hand. Through stars of pain, Eamon feels something in his mouth. The mate recoils to stare at his maimed hand.

This gives Eamon a second to roll over to a low crouch. He spits out the first joint of a finger. The crew leans in a little closer to see the bloody stub. As he tries to draw breath and stand, his broken ribs stab him. His body's pain is welcome compared to the agony his heart cannot escape. He grimaces. "That's right. Kill me! Please."

"If dyin' is what you want . . ."

"I WANT NOTHING! There's nothing left to want. You can't kill me because you already did when you took me from my family."

"But you don't want it to hurt."

"Ha! You jest!" To even the mate's surprise, Eamon laughs and points to his own bloodied face. "*This* is not pain. This is nothing. I'm already dead, and I'm takin' you with me."

Eamon lunges to take his opponent over the side of the ship. Even if he gets his arms wrapped around the mate, it will be like trying to tackle a tree. The mate assumes nothing now. He has enough room to box instead of wrestle. Eamon feels impaled by the first blow to his body. His breath leaves him as an involuntary scream. The next punch snaps his head back. His legs buckle, but he doesn't fall before the mate kicks him in the crotch. He lands on a hatch to one of the ship's holds. There, the mate pummels him with fists like mallets. Eamon tries to cover his face. His perception slows. Oddly distant from the now mutilated tissue of his face, he hears the sound of facial bones breaking. His ears ring; one bleeds. *How long can this go on?* he thinks. *Has there ever been anything else?* A grip grabs him by the throat. The mate kneels on his broken chest. He glimpses the mate's other hand with a knife poised above him, but he can't let go of the hand at his throat. Eamon is suffocating. The last thing he hears is the mate snarling. "Dead men don't need eyeballs."

What he doesn't hear is another voice, commanding, "MISTER DUNCAN, *that* will be enough!"

CHAPTER 3

THE FORECASTLE HATCH slides open, letting in a blast of rain and wind. Jack's bulk darkens the opening as he climbs from the deck down the companionway ladder. At the bottom rung, he reaches up and slides the hatch shut. Stepping down to the cabin sole, he turns to face forward. At his back, aft of the ladder, is a bulkhead across the width of the ship. To either side of him, bins and benches are built next to the hull. The base of the foremast, like a large tree grown through the center of the room, pierces through the deck overhead and the sole at his feet. Lashed to the mast is a water cask. Forward of that, a crowd of hammocks swing in unison, most of them empty. The space is almost forty feet long and thirty feet wide but tapers toward the bow. There isn't enough headroom for Jack to stand tall. The air is stagnant, rotten, and damp. Two gimballed whale-oil lamps dimly light the space, casting wild shadows as they rock with the ship's motion.

The cabin is noisy with the sound of waves crashing past. Two men who have come off watch already snore in their hammocks. They sleep in their oil skins rather than struggle in and out of them each time they go on deck. It's a leaky deck. Still, the shelter it gives is welcome. A few men sit on the leeward bench to dry off.

Jack stands for a minute to shake off the water that clings to him. Making up his mind, he pulls off his rain gear and hangs it on hooks where other coats and pants look like ghosts as they sway with the ships motion. A couple of threadbare towels hang there too. He wrings one out to wipe himself off. His eyes adapt to the darkness. His hearing adjusts from the high pitch of the wind to the deep thunder of the sea going by. Now, if only his nose would get used to the stench. He ducks the deck beams to make his way to the dim light of a lamp. Under its glow, Sam sits on a small barrel, watching Eamon's unconscious form in a hammock.

Jack raises his voice. In fresh weather, there is no such thing as a quiet conversation here. "How'd he do while we were on deck?"

"His fever's passed," Sam half shouts.

"Will he wake up soon?"

"I don't know. He breathes so shallow. I took off the wrappings around his chest. Maybe that will help."

"Have mercy, look at him." Jack shakes his head. "His face all purple and yellow and swollen twice the size it should be. How would ya even know if he opened his eyes? Did the mate say anythin' when ya doctored his finger?"

"Only that there's no use in me fixin' Eamon, that he'll be dead before he can set foot on shore."

"At least the crew is scared of him. As long as they think he's a madman, they'll keep their distance from him." Jack watches Sam squeeze water out of a rag onto Eamon's lips. "Where did ya learn to doctor like this?"

"I'm treatin' him like I would a farm animal." Sam shrugs. "Just guessin' and common sense. Strange, some of the crew are asking me about their pains too."

"Ya could do worse. They're callin' ya 'Doc,' which is lucky if ya play it right. 'Course, you're big enough they'd think twice about layin' for ya." Jack reaches for what looks like a rag out of a hammock. "Do ya think the dead man's shirt will fit him?"

"Close enough. What's it been now, four days?"

"No, it's barely three."

Sam shakes his head and Jack goes on. "It takes a while to get used to standin' yer watches. Can ya keep any food down?"

"Some of that hard tack is still with me, but I feel weak, not like myself at all. I'm a farmer, Jack. My whole life is about the ground beneath my feet, which there's none of now. I can tell you about soil and seasons and planting, but I'm worthless out here. Out of sight of land! I never imagined this. I keep staring at the horizon before I realize I'm looking for a shore. The only ground out here is the bottom of the sea, and how far down is that? Not to think what's down there. It could drive me mad, too, like Eamon."

"Don't let it show. Give yerself some time. Hell, yer not worthless if yer our doc."

A farmer's experience is bizarre at sea. To counter his confusion, Sam helps Cook with the livestock: a half-dozen chickens, a pig, and a couple goats, all in cages lashed down behind the foredeck. The eggs, meat, and goat's milk are for the captain and officers alone. The rest of the crew live on salted meat, biscuits, and grog. If they have produce, it's potatoes and onions or the officers' leftovers, stirred into a mush. Only on Sundays do they get a sweet pudding.

Sam is accustomed to hard work from before sunrise to after sunset. At home, unless livestock is birthing, he counts upon a solid night's sleep. Now he is on deck every four hours, even in the middle of the night. In heavy weather, he's often back on deck for part of his off-watch. It's driving him to fatigue. Sleep is a small comfort since it's filled with nightmares, and waking is another nightmare itself. Lord help him when his part includes "going aloft." So far, the captain and mates have kept him pulling lines on deck and learning to steer.

Coop, on the other hand, has already climbed to the top of the rigging. At sixteen, he is used to being told what to do. He adapts rapidly and feels pushed to learn everything as fast as he can. His sense of wonder and fear, his scramble to preserve his skin, these eclipse his losses. While he misses his family and friends, he could not have imagined anything except the yoke of their presumptions. He was the cooper's son; of course, he would apprentice with his father and inherit the trade. Until this strangest turn of events, the staves and hoops of barrels were to be his life's work. Now his place in the world is a challenge that spans the horizon, a challenge to which he rises as naturally as the ship's bow crests over each wave. He can't admit it to himself yet, but he welcomes the adventure.

Coop gravitates to helping the ship's carpenter, a short, sturdy, old man of few words, strong arms, and big hands. He has a Nova Scotian accent, and his name has long since been lost when it was supplanted by that of all ship's carpenters: "Chips." Working with wood offers no shortcuts, and there are many barrels for cargo and provisions. He is glad for Coop's inheritance.

Coop's mates slap his back at the small victory of hauling a line together to trim or hoist a sail. Surprised at his own grin, he wipes it from his face. There is a power he never imagined swirling around him. He senses he is part of something large now. Coop never met anyone like these men. Pocked and ragged, with no society to rein them in, they do not impress, yet their feats from aloft to deep in the bilge leave him panting to catch up. He hasn't learned to time his efforts with the roll of the ship, something the men don't even know they do but are training him to. Without speaking, they challenge him to match their work. Their derision and laughter sound light, but beneath its tone, he knows he is being tested.

By contrast, the first mate is impatient and cuffs Coop often. Coop can't believe the man's size and force. It is beyond him how Eamon survived that fight. And the man's voice! He can be heard the length of the ship even in dirty weather. In the first mate's watch, Coop is on deck while Jack and Sam are below with the second watch and next to Eamon's hammock.

"Is his jaw broken?" Jack asks. "If he wakes, he'll need to eat."

"He lost a few teeth, but his jaw's fine. And he's taken a bit of water."

"Y'know, he might not want to live, but we could use another hand. Ever since a British frigate boarded her at sea and stole half her men, she's been short of crew. That's why they shanghaied us. She's a big ship in her prime. At least a hundred and seventy feet, six hundred tons, and over-rigged. Beyond the waisters, we're only"—he counts to himself—"twenty of us, not including Eamon and the old man."

"Old man?" Sam asks.

At first, Jack frowns at Sam's confusion. "Ah, no. Every captain is called 'the old man.' He's no older than I am."

"How many more men would you want?"

"I'd as soon have twice as many."

"Waisters?"

"Those are the men who don't normally haul away or go aloft: Cook, Chips, and Swede the sailmaker. Then there's the bosun, mates, and the old man. Being short on crew makes for spacious quarters here, but ten to a watch isn't enough. That's why you're so tired. They have to call us on deck when we should be off." He feels the ship's motion and reaches up to a beam overhead. "A cross sea is comin', hold on."

As the ship slews, Sam falls off the keg and watches it roll a short way. When it rolls back, he grabs it, rights it, and sits back on it while Jack holds the bowl and cloth he was using. "What's this cabin called?"

"Fo'c'sle. Short for forecastle. Forward of the masts and imagine calling *this* a castle. Proves there's a sense of humor. 'Tis the roughest place on the ship. Even the rats live aft of here."

"Have you found out where we're goin'?"

"Captains like to keep their crew guessin', and none of us can read enough to tell, but it looks like we're headed 'round the Horn. Cook saw Chinese writin' on some papers."

"The captain can read Chinese?"

"Oh, hell no, I'm sure not."

A mumble startles them both. "Wud jew say?"

"Whoa! Ahoy there." Jack looks at Eamon. "Are ya back aboard, mate? Among the livin'."

"Eamon! You can hear us?"

"I can 'ear you. On'y a little though." He gasps. "I saw your lips movin'." Tears start down from the corners of his eyes.

Sam unwraps a bandage from Eamon's head and pulls cotton wadding out of one ear. "Can you hear me now?"

"Tha's better, but I hear ringin' too." Eamon winces.

"Where do you hurt?" Sam asks. "The most, I mean."

Eamon raises a hand to feel his pains. "All . . . all over. In my chest, I guess. Or my neck. Ouch! Oh, and my nose."

"Are ya hungry?" Jack asks.

"No, feel sick. Dizzy. Thought I might be dead. S'prised the captain didn't finish me off."

"The captain? It's the captain who saved you," Sam tells him.

"Af'er I bit 'is finger off?" Eamon slurs through swollen lips.

In the shadows of the forecastle, there are a few chuckles from the crew who have been listening. As their interest grows, the distance they keep shrinks.

"No, Eamon," Jack explains, "that was the chief mate. And he *would* have killed ya if the captain hadn't ordered him to stop."

"S'prised he obeyed."

"There was the small matter of a pistol in the captain's hand. And lucky for you, he needs every crewman he can get. By rights, he could hang you for fightin' an officer."

"Lucky? You're not serious."

"Eamon, don't start down that road again." Jack's tone is harsh. "I'm tellin' ya, it makes ya crazy. Give it up, or don't bother wakin' up. D'ya hear me?"

Sam keeps checking Eamon's injuries, not confident that consciousness has anything to do with recovery. For all he knows, Eamon is waking up to watch his own demise.

"Ouch!" Another wince. "Sam, when do you think I'll be able to take a decent breath?"

"As bad as it smells in here, you might not want to. And I'd have a better chance of answering that if you were a cow. I'm a farmer. Remember?"

"A cow would know better than to get into that fight, eh?"

Something between a grin and a grimace opens a split on Eamon's lip.

"Easy, Eamon. You're makin' more work for me. What do you say? It'd be good to get some food in you."

Eamon nods as he touches the swollen landscape of his face.

"If ya can call this slop food," Jack adds. "It might kill ya if the mate doesn't."

Coop's wet face comes into view above Eamon. He's been given a hat, and drops drip from its broad brim. "Eamon, I heard you woke up after all! Jack's holdin' our bets on that. And if you *did* wake up, when?"

Jack and Sam shake their heads at the boy's candid report.

Eamon asks, "What are you staring at?"

"You ought to be glad you can't see yourself . . ." Coop answers.

"Whoa, Coop," Jack warns, "don't be scarin' our new recruit. Go see what Cook's got that he'll not need to chew."

"Sure. Welcome back, Eamon, I think."

"I already said that." Jack spins Coop around and pushes him aft. "Now go on, and don't come back without somethin' he can eat."

Sam studies the swollen slits where he should see Eamon's eyes. "So, Eamon, here's my best guess. You've lost some hearing in one ear, and a few teeth. At least you still have eyes. You've gained some scars and a broken nose. The swelling on your face will go down. You have a few broken ribs, but you're not spittin' up blood. So, it doesn't seem they've poked a hole in anything. For a while there, you had a fever, but it's gone now. I got a little water in you, but you need more. Maybe after you keep some food down, you'll start feelin' better. If not"—Sam pauses—"I don't know what else to do for you. What I'm sayin' is that you're not out of the dark yet."

As it turns out, Eamon recovers, but Sam is right. He isn't out of the dark by any means.

CHAPTER 4

"COME IN." CAPTAIN Rolinson answers the knock on his cabin door.

The door swings open, and Eamon's swollen face peers in. His posture is stooped, and his breath is shallow. He steps in, closes the door, and holds onto its handle to steady himself. He clears his throat, cautious to whatever is about to play out. Eamon doesn't know what to expect—from the captain or himself. *Will some weapon come to hand again? Will I attack the captain? How is it that I attacked the first mate?* His defiance is hampered by his wounds and, more so, by hopelessness.

At first, all Eamon sees is a full head of white hair bent over a mess of papers. These papers cover a large, heavy, and ornate table in the middle of the cabin. A weathered hand automatically reaches a quill to an ink well in the corner of the table and returns to the page. As the captain continues without looking up, Eamon maintains his balance and details come into focus. On the back wall of the room, a bench seat is below a half dozen windows letting in shaded light. A middle one is open, and the quiet sound of the ship's wake pours in. At one corner window is a small, polished brass cannon in its carriage; at the other, a globe is cradled in a waist-high stand. A generous and neatly tucked bunk is built-in to the portside of the room. Drawers are fitted below it. Open curtains frame it. Forward of this is a closet and more drawers, and forward of that is a closed door. To the starboard side of the cabin is a bookshelf. Leather-bound volumes are kept on the shelf by a thin piece of wood halfway up their spines and spanning the length of the shelf. Three chairs hang from hooks lower on that wall. The door where Eamon stands is centered on the forward bulkhead of the captain's cabin. To one side of where he stands, a suit of oilskins and a linen towel hang on hooks. The shine of metal stops his scan: a wash basin is attached to the bulkhead, with a looking glass above it. To the other side, a spyglass hangs by its lanyard. From another hook, a scabbard hangs, the handle of a saber atop it. Two large sea chests are along the base of the wall, each with a lock on its hasp. One lock is open. Eamon notices at each table leg a ringbolt in the deck with a taut line to it. All the furniture is either built-in or tied down so that it cannot crash about in rough weather, yet it can also be loosed and moved easily. A raised lip at three edges of the table keeps things from sliding off. No doubt there is a lashing under the captain's chair too. The lashings, though, cannot hide the sense of motion. Curtains sway, gimbaled lamps rock, and the creaking of the ship and the sound of the sea going by prove the nature of the space.

Two scratching sounds loom into Eamon's foreground: the quill on paper and the scabbard wearing an arc into the bulkhead as it swings. A hatch above the table lets light into the otherwise shaded room. Eamon is struck by the fresh air, the quiet of the sea slipping astern and the gentleness of the motion compared to the stench, roar, and thrashing in the forecastle. This, the light from the hatch and the captain's piercing blue eyes, gives him the sudden feeling that he is coming out of a fog.

"Jesus, look at you. You'll not be fit to go aloft for weeks. At least the weather's eased, and you can start slow enough." The captain studies him. "I understand that you were a printer ashore."

The captain's use of past tense trips Eamon's attention, but he manages to answer, "Yes, yes, I am."

The captain pitches his voice low and menacing. "You will use 'sir' when you answer me, or I will add to your wounds. Is that understood?" It isn't a question yet demands an answer.

"Yes," Eamon replies. The captain waits. " . . . sir."

"There is a vast distance between us and for good reason. Mine is solitary business. By necessity." The captain stops himself from going on. "I assume that a printer can read and write."

"Of course. Sir."

"And are you equipped with basic bookkeeping?"

"To an extent that will run a business." The room seems silent, waiting. "Sir."

"Very well. As you can tell from this mess"—the captain stands up from his chair and waves his hand at the tabletop—"there's more to sailing a ship than what you see on deck. I have no purser now, and paperwork is not the chief mate's strength. With too few crew, I need him on deck anyway." He stretches to relieve the stiffness of sitting too long. "I am forced to adhere to manifests more than in the past. What was once sealed with a handshake has been replaced with contracts that themselves are hard to trust. On your daylight watches, you'll square away these papers like I square away this ship. If I hand her over proper to her new owners, I should keep command of her. After all, she is good and fast."

"This ship's been sold, sir?"

"Aye, she has. By all accounts, to a good company, though it hails from Hong Kong. We shall see when we get there. Until then, we have a long way to go and plenty of ports where we can add to our fortune. In the meantime, your job will be to survive and right these papers. Surviving won't be easy with the mate layin' for you, but I've put you into the second watch, and I've given Mister Duncan orders to leave you be."

Eamon can't manage to say thanks. The captain goes on, "That doesn't mean you'll not come to grief anyway. Many men have been lost at sea, mysteriously or not. You'll work as hard as every other man and need to watch your back. You couldn't survive another round with the mate, but I doubt it will come to that. Comin' from a man of war, he respects nothing if not orders."

"We're not a man of war, sir?" Eamon's inclusive use of the plural feels strange on his tongue. "Aren't they the ones who shanghai men?"

The captain cannot comprehend the extent of Eamon's ignorance. *Has he not noticed no marines and no gun deck?* "They get most of the blame, but no, we're a merchant ship."

In league with whores and innkeepers, it isn't hard for a ship to send her toughs to shore and drag new crew off to sea. Unions and laws to protect and instruct the crew are decades away. A captain metes out his law however he sees fit, brutality more the rule than the exception. Though they won't admit it, like all kings, captains fear losing their throne. They have witnessed the poverty and degradation of their equals ashore. A captain without a command is a lost soul, and there are many ways to lose one's ship. Beyond storms and reefs, mutineers and pirates, there is the business of running a ship. Whether the dangers faced are nautical or economic, they arise from forces beyond a captain's control. At best, the variables keep life interesting, or, at worst, they kill.

"May I ask . . . sir, where we are?"

The captain follows Eamon's gaze to where the globe stands. In the navy, it is a capital crime for an officer to reveal a ship's position or teach navigation to anyone but a cadet. If men don't know where they are or how to navigate, what good will mutiny be to them? For the same reason, even without a law, keeping these secrets extends to merchantmen as well. Even so, crews are adept at guessing the next port of call, and soon this printer will be privy to more than most men. "We're in the middle of the North Atlantic. We will soon leave Bermuda astern."

"Could you show me, on the globe . . . sir?"

Eamon knows nothing of the depth of his request. The captain narrows his gaze but goes to the globe anyway. His upright posture and confident gait are a sharp contrast to Eamon's aching steps and unsteady balance. Enroute, Eamon grips the back of the captain's chair for a moment. A holster strapped there holds a flintlock pistol.

First the saber, and now this? If I had grabbed the saber, he would have shot me. And if I grab this? But Jack is right, it's too late. I'm too tired, too weak, too slow. I can't kill anyone. All this flashes through his mind in an instant.

The captain watches Eamon's attention catch on the pistol. Of all the variables he deals with, the nature of his crew is the most curious. Other than the weather, his crew's mood bears the most on the ship's profitability. A happy crew requires far less command and takes pride in that fact. The result is a ship that stays in better repair and sails faster. In port, she loads better, carries more cargo, and departs sooner. None of which the first mate understands and all of which seem like past luxuries. As he waits, the captain wonders if Eamon will ever fully recover. Still, he senses underlying coordination which he thinks implies intelligence. Eamon arrives at the globe and holds on to a beam over head while the captain points.

"We're out here. That's Bermuda. Those big islands, south and west of our course, are Cuba and Haiti. The string of little ones are the Indies."

"Will we see them? Sir?"

"No. They're well off our rhumb line, and who knows what's left of the pirates that raid from there. The Spanish and French have their hands full pretending to own any of them, and Britain is laying claim to what they can. The more remote areas belong to natives and runaway slaves. 'Tis all too much politics. Our next landfall should be in the Pacific if the doldrums and the Horn are decent to us."

Eamon scans the globe to orient himself and find his way home. He startles at the loud clang of the ship's bell close above the hatch. It rings in four pair. Soon, he hears a distant voice call out, "We've got six knots, Mister Duncan, sir."

"Six knots at eight bells" booms out from above. "Helmsman?"

"Course is south-southeast, sir."

"South-southeast it is."

The captain leaves Eamon standing at the globe and goes back to the table. He pens something into an open book, after which he massages his hands and mutters, "Well enough, if the trade winds aren't overdue." He looks up. "You'll join your watch now. I'm done with you. Report back after the noon sight tomorrow."

"Yes, sir. Will there be something to see at noon tomorrow?"

Confusion is a rare expression to cross the captain's face. It gives way when he once more understands Eamon's inexperience. "Bugger you and your questions. Get out and go ask your mates." After Eamon is gone, the captain shakes his head and chuffs a small laugh. "'Something to see at noon,' save me from landlubbers."

CHAPTER 5

BEYOND KEEPING HIS distance from the chief mate, Eamon's focus is on his own balance and fatigue. Often seasick, he grows feeble in the first week. When he retches, he feels stabbed by his broken ribs. It's all he can do to get through each immediate task. In the second week, he keeps food down. At night, sleep is his hope for recovery but is often lost when more hands are called on deck. It isn't until the third week that he begins to regain strength and stamina. After that, what suffers most are his hands. Jack promises that after they blister and bleed, they will callous. To demonstrate, he strikes a match off his own palm to light his pipe.

Eamon is challenged by the language that surrounds him. A rope isn't a rope; it's a "line." There are, in fact, miles of lines, each with its own name and purpose. They're not the rat's nest they appear to be but an intricate and evolved web between three masts and the deck. The mainmast is one hundred forty feet tall! Let the wrong line go, and the result can be fatal to someone in the rigging. There are braces and halyards, buntlines and earrings, stays and shrouds, controlling a cloud of countless sails, literally acres of them, each with its own name as well. "Up" and "down," more than vertical descriptions, are about the ship's course relative to the wind's direction. Their synonyms are "close to" and "off" the wind. A north wind isn't going north; it's coming from the north. The "landscape" on deck includes deadeyes and scuppers, bulwarks and bulkheads, goosenecks and knightheads, ad infinitum.

All of which must be maintained. In daylight hours, every

crewman attends a chore at all times, interrupted only when taking a turn at the helm or for a change of sail. Tasks include sewing sails, serving and parceling line, tarring rigging, making baggywrinkles, standing watch, etcetera. Then there are the decks to "stone" every morning and always the bilge to pump. After supper, the men off watch play dice and cards, smoke, scribe scrimshaw, and mend their clothes. Otherwise, they rest up for their next watch.

Climbing the rigging and pulling lines, pumping the bilge and steering, and simply balancing are continuous and keep a crew strong. Sam has always been big and strapping, but with a sailor's diet and exercise, he's already a stone lighter. Where the crew's weaknesses reveal themselves is near the equator, when *Atalanta* is in the heat and calm of the doldrums. Every sailor prefers battling a storm to waiting for the wind. With no wind, ocean swells start a ship rolling side to side. Taut rigging works loose and must be retightened and tuned. If empty sails are left set, they flog back and forth until they tear. The crew is forever up and down in the rigging, chasing the least patch of wind. They get their hopes up when *Atalanta* begins to move, only to have them dashed within a mile when her speed dies. Then it's aloft again to furl the same sails they just set. Working to exhaustion to go nowhere drives a sailor mad.

After five days of calm, the men feel the doldrums like a grip upon them: suffocating and fatal if they can't break free before scurvy starts. The surface of the sea is so flat that its reflection of the sky makes the horizon disappear. Sometimes the ship is so still that she feels more aground than afloat. Jack calls it "an oily sea." During the day, the men work in shade where they can find it. Too hot below, at night, they sleep on the sails on deck. Everyone keeps an eye out for a squall that might cross their path and bring wind.

When the next order comes, it's cursed. "Mister Duncan, Mister Strom, by now we have a crop of barnacles and worms slowing us down. Rig lines over the sides so a man in the water has something to hold onto. Chips has tools for the men. Have them scrape off as much as they can reach. The worst of it will be at the waterline. Watch for sharks and arm two men with muskets. Be ready to pull the swimmers out. If we manage a little more speed from the next wind, maybe we can get free of this."

Sam is quick to step up to the second mate. "Mister Strom, sir. May I be one to carry a musket? I'm not lazy, but I can't swim."

"Aye, Sam. I know you're not lazy, but are you good with a musket?"

"Sir, I've done my share of hunting."

"Very well, the bosun will give you a musket. Load it and be ready."

"Thank you, sir."

Coop climbs down a rope ladder, eyeing the water warily. But after feeling baked on deck, he declares the water a relief.

The work is brutal. *Atalanta* seems too big an adversary, covered with barnacles. As she rolls with the swell, she thrashes and scratches the men. When the first watch gets out of the water with no sign of a shark, they go on lookout for the second watch. Eamon's injuries still limit him, but he's ordered into the water anyway. The work dizzies him, and he vomits seawater he hasn't intended to swallow. Back aboard, exhausted, the crew admits that they all smell better.

This night, as if it can only happen unseen in the dark, *Atalanta* catches a whisper of wind. Captain and crew hold their breath, setting one sail after another. The chuckle of water passing by the hull is their reward. By morning, the men feel they are indeed stealing away, albeit at just three knots, and they credit the captain and clean hull with their escape.

Eamon is as relieved as any of them until Jack laughs and tells him, "The old man says we'll cross the equator in the mornin'. So, ya best get ready to meet Neptune."

"'Meet Neptune?' What are you on about?"

"You've not sailed across the equator before, have ya?"

"Certainly not."

"That means you're a pollywog, but tomorrow, by rites, you'll be a shellback. 'Tis no less than a caterpillar becomin' a butterfly. Once you're a shellback, you're a real sailor. You're one of us. And no one can take it away from ya."

"Grow up, man." Eamon gives Jack a sideways look. "I'll never be a sailor. I don't belong here."

"But *y'are* here. Regardless of what or who y'are, you're here. In the middle of the ocean about to cross the equator. Neptune will christen even you. And ya don't want to run afoul of the rest of the crew. We'll bring you and Sam and Coop into an honor we're proud of. Hell, you've sailed across an ocean. You've seen and done things no pollywog will ever see or do. Don't tarnish our standing amongst ourselves. And don't worry, I'll watch yer back for ya."

"Jack, why am I not comforted by that?"

The next day, the captain and officers look down from their domain: the quarterdeck. The ceremony will take place on the main deck. The physical and mental boundaries between them and the crew are unspoken but clear: the captain, officers, and cook have free rein of the entire ship, but they work on the quarterdeck and live in the aft cabins; the crew inhabits the main and foredeck and crosses aft only when ordered; a crewman never addresses his superiors before being addressed. If he initiates a conversation, he peppers the dialog with "sir," and the only acceptable subject is the ship and the sailing of her.

Swede is dressed as mighty Neptune. He sits upon an improvised throne. His crown is made of canvas, painted gold and studded with seashells as jewels. He holds a harpoon as a trident. His countenance is stern. To his side sits Chips dressed as his queen. A wig of rope strands cascades from beneath his, or her, crown. He cradles a dead fish swaddled as the "royal babe." Several of the crew, Jack among them, dress as mermaids. They wear wigs and skirts of rope and pairs of coconut shells tied to their chests.

The three initiates emerge from the crew's companionway blindfolded. They're splashed with buckets of rotten galley scraps that Cook, as a matter of course, saved for the ceremony. Ordered to lick up what they can and mop the rest with their shirts, Eamon,

Coop, and Sam go to their hands and knees. The shellbacks berate and interrogate them mercilessly.

"Can you keep the secrets of the deep?"

"You aren't worthy!"

"Will you defend to the death the honor of all shellbacks?"

"Who are you that Neptune should let you live?"

All three suffer their hair shorn badly. Their blindfolds removed, lukewarm pine tar is painted onto their faces and chests. Commanded to rub onto themselves a stinky mix of ship worms and seaweed scraped from *Atalanta's* bottom the day before, Coop enthuses, Sam laughs, and Eamon humbles himself.

"Don't you dare get to your feet! Pollywogs must approach the throne on their knees. Kneel before Neptune! Do not incur his wrath."

They arrive to kiss Neptune's feet. The king of the oceans ridicules them and at last recites their duties as his subjects. "Promise your loyalty to me, the deep blue sea and all our brothers upon it," he commands. "And now, kiss the royal babe." After this, he touches his trident to each of them, proclaiming, "I hereby dub you a member of the mighty shellbacks!" They are then drenched with buckets of seawater, clapped on their backs, and welcomed as citizens of the sea. The captain kindly follows this with a ration of grog for all.

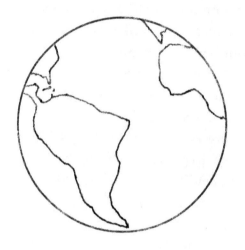

CHAPTER 6

LATE ONE GLORIOUS afternoon, *Atalanta's* rigging is taut and humming. Diamonds of sunlight dance off the waves all the way to the western horizon. The blue dome of the sky is punctuated by white cloud cathedrals. Though she is tiny on the ocean's surface, up close, a ship with all sails set appears as towering as the clouds. Her bow wave roars, falls astern, and disappears in a hiss. The air is fresh, and the crew is content. Each man attends his assigned duty. They jabber back and forth. Their rations have been full. The ship is driving well, and they are proud of her. All of this is wasted on Eamon. His gaze is intent on the compass as he tries to steady a course. He sweats while working the steering wheel. A man stands close at hand, ready to step in and keep the course from straying too far.

"Sail ho!" Coop's voice comes down from high in the rigging. Eamon looks up to find the boy, though a forest of sails makes it impossible. "Ahoy on deck, sail ho!" comes again. Eamon brings his gaze back to the horizon and compass. The crew pauses, and the decks become quiet.

"Where away?" bellows Mister Strom as he scans the horizon.

"Off our larboard quarter. Umm, three points forward of our stern? Or five points abaft our beam. Is that right, sir?"

A chuckle from the men on deck is tense.

"You tell me, young Coop! You're the bloody lookout," the second mate calls back. Voice low now, he says, "Spanky, lay aloft. I don't want to roust the old man if that pup's chasin' whitecaps again. Take my glass with you."

The man who stood by to help Eamon takes the proffered telescope, drapes its lanyard across his shoulders, and vanishes up into the sails. Even after some weeks, Eamon marvels that Spanky climbs the rigging as casually as he walks the deck. *Part ape,* he thinks.

The second mate calls the bosun over. "Are the stuns'ls ready?"

"Aye, Mister Strom, they are."

"If there's a sail out there, we could be on the run. We can't engage anyone."

"No, sir, we can't. Maybe we should carry more than our few guns."

It is the captain that answers as he comes up on deck, in shirtsleeves and with spyglass in hand, "And how shall we pay for a gunnery, Gates? Practice is expensive, and without it, cannons are no use. We would kill more of us than them."

"Begging your pardon sir, but enough of us served in the navy to teach the others."

"We barely have enough crew to sail and certainly not enough to fight. If someone comes for us, you best hope we can outrun them."

"Aye, sir."

The captain makes his way to the weather rail. He grips a shroud while he scans the horizon. To the muttering that drifts down, he shouts up into the rigging, "Should we send your hammock up, Spanky, or is a ship out there?"

A voice comes down. "No, sir, I'm . . . I'm tryin' to steady this glass to be sure."

"I'm not asking for her hailing port or the color of their eyes."

"Aye, sir. There's a ship. Three masts. Her hull is still well down. She's straight out on our larboard quarter."

The captain snaps his own glass open and up in one motion. His view shaped round, he scans along the horizon to see if his eye will trip over anything. Then back again slowly. Most of the crew has made their way to the ship's gunwale now. The edge of the earth holds their future beyond their stare, but it always has. Shaking his head, the captain lowers his telescope and admits, "I don't see anything. An extra ration of grog for the boy if they don't give chase."

"Stuns'ls and royals, sir?"

"Stuns'ls, but wait on the royals until after dark. The late sun lights their sails bright while ours are in silhouette. Let's not wave our tallest sails at them."

"Aye, sir."

"Helmsman . . ."

By the time their eyes meet, Eamon realizes that the helmsman is himself and that any pause in answering is longer than expected. "Sir?"

"Our course, what is it?"

Eamon looks down and finds he is again off course. He looks back up in some confusion. Should he report what his course is supposed to be or what it currently is? "Southeast, sir, by a bit south."

"A bit south? Mister Strom, put someone on the helm who can steady our course. Bring her up to southeast. We will wait until dark to make a course change and then work to weather of them. With luck, dark will come on before they see us. We'll know in the morning. Cook will keep supper until the stuns'ls are set."

"Yes, sir." The second turns and calls for all hands. The first mate arrives on deck and takes over while the second hauls lines along with the men. As Eamon comes off the helm, Jack meets him and mutters for him to stay close. While they work, the rigging's hum rises a pitch, and the decks slant a bit more. Dusk is falling when half the crew goes below to eat. Before Coop's call from the masthead, their ease and chatter seemed part of the air they breathed. It's replaced now by a determined calm and will not return until they are beyond the immediate danger. Even from his oblivion, Eamon feels the change. Its hush and tension leave him confused, but he is getting used to that.

"Chips! Shutter all ports," the captain orders. "Light only the essential lanterns besides one in my cabin and one in the galley. We'll run dark tonight."

"Yes, sir."

They might find themselves sailing for their lives in the morning, but the captain has no intention of waiting until then. If there is a chase on, the crew might as well get used to it sooner instead of later. It is dark when the second watch finishes eating. The old man calls for the royals and a new course.

The captain's orders become a bond between himself and the crew, a bond he will call upon this night. He takes their blood and sweat, their fear and resentment, and invests it in an unknown future taking shape now. The crew's duties, in the rigging and sails, in the smallest details—they all add up to this moment. Is *Atalanta* ready to be pushed to her limits? Will there be a weak link? Did someone cheat his task? The account the captain will bank upon is the ship's speed.

The only sleep anyone gets this night will be on deck, hunkered against a bulwark or cabin top and between orders. There will be no sails to curl up on since the old man intends to fly them all. When men work like this, the ship becomes an extension of them. They, in turn, become part of the ship and its rigging. With sight less dominant in the dark, other senses take over and boundaries blur. Water rushes past, night goes on, and men grow tired. Unwitting, they transfer more of their grip from themselves to the ship and the captain's intent. They tune to details they assumed before: the deck's slant, the rumble of the ship's bow wave, a sail out of trim, and a line less taut. They anticipate orders; thus, officers bark fewer of them and those more quietly.

When the chief mate calls for the mizzen staysails, Swede, as the sailmaker, mutters, "There's lightning out there."

Jack agrees. "We'll have to strike them if we get into a squall."

At each bell, the men listen for the report from the officer on deck. "Eight bells and steady at nine knots, sir." They scan the black horizon out of habit. The ship sighted before sunset grows in their imaginations, threatening to appear from anywhere at any time.

Real threats grow more immediate when their course looks bound to cross with a thunderstorm. A quadrant of the sky is starless, lit by frequent flashes of lightning. Not wanting to lose any distance from the other ship, the captain waits to reduce sail. The crew stands by, half of them already aloft. He orders the studding sails taken in. Then the skysails and royals furled. The ship's roaring wake audibly eases.

The local wind is sucked up into the approaching monster. The ship's forward motion through stagnant air puts the sails aback. Rigging groans in protest. Staysails luff, thrashing their blocks and sheets.

"There'll be a blast out of this," Jack tells Eamon. "Hell's about to break loose."

"But the wind's gone."

"Have ya not heard of the calm before a storm?"

The captain's tone reflects the approaching menace. "Mister Duncan, strike and stow the flying jib NOW. Mister Strom, aft stays'ls, t'gallants next, and the courses last. We'll keep the tops'ls, and fore stays'l only. Helmsman, bring your course to south. There will be a new wind on us."

"Aye, sir, south it is."

In the calm, the mates merely speak their orders to be heard. Jack and Eamon, among the crew on deck, scramble from pinrail to pinrail. They put a fathom of slack in sheets, clewlines, and buntlines and ease halyards while the men in the rigging clew up and furl sails. A streak of lightning illuminates *Atalanta* and her rigging, followed closely by a BOOM! The thunder rolls away, echoing into the distance.

The other sound is the mate's voice urging all speed. "Hurry, you monkeys. Damn your eyes; get down to the courses!"

The next flash reveals the upper sails furled. Men hasten down to the lower yards. Big rain drops fall sparsely. A sound like distant cavalry draws Eamon's eyes over his shoulder. Nothing can be seen in that direction. The black there is complete.

"Helmsman," the captain orders, "southwest now, if she'll answer. Hard over."

"Aye, sir, southwest."

"This is it," Jack tells Eamon. "Hold on."

Eamon wraps an arm around one of the shrouds.

The first gust strikes as if it is a huge fist. Even with few sails set, *Atalanta* staggers under the blow. How a man in the rigging can hang on is beyond Eamon. He's glad Jack led him to the windward rail; the lee rail is under water. It looks to Eamon that the ship is capsizing. Driven rain obscures the bow from the stern and stings exposed skin, forcing men to face away from it. The wind tastes salty. The helmsman cannot stop the ship from rounding up closer to the wind. There's a loud crack above their heads and some rigging goes slack while other strains more. Sails luffing so hard sound like gunfire. There are desperate shouts. Another flash of lightning burns a scene of chaos into Eamon's memory. Thunder completes the impression that this is a battle. Is the other ship firing upon them? Another flash, he sees the wavetops blowing off into mist and the rain beating flat what's left. The chief mate joins the helmsman at the wheel, and slowly the decks come back from their insane slant. Where whispers carried moments ago, shouts must be bellowed into someone's ear to be heard. Jack tugs at Eamon's arm to follow aft along the rail. Swede and Johnny meet them with a large block and tackle. While Jack and Eamon lash one block to the quarter cleat on the bulwarks, Swede and Johnny struggle up the mizzen rat lines, alternately climbing and handing the second block up, each to the other. More men arrive. At a signal, they heave on the tackle and pin it in place.

Lightning shows the few jibs and fore topsails still holding. The main topsail has torn, and men are gathering it in before it tears further. Eamon is aghast that this cataclysm is a matter of course. The captain stands by the windward rail at the quarter as if rooted. Variously, a mate or the bosun confers with him and brings new orders to the men.

Sam is now the second man at the helm. His eyes wide, he shouts, "THIS WHEEL IS ALIVE!"

"WHAT?" Eamon calls back. Unwilling to leave where he holds on, he half reads Sam's lips.

Jack explains, "It's the rush of water on the rudder, like holdin' the reins on a team of wild horses."

Eamon leans in to shout, "How fast are we going?"

"All of thirteen knots, maybe more. And with cargo, pushin' near a thousand ton."

All sense of time is lost. After the first rush, minutes feel like hours. The men know only the task before them, trusting it to lead to the next task more than to another dawn. A magic takes place. The ship becomes their conduit to the storm, the ocean, and their futures. Even the most callous among them has become part of something beyond himself and the ship. Near dawn, the storm's echoes sound victorious as it leaves *Atalanta* in its wake. In relative peace, she resumes her course.

The men travel back from the storm's spell on the captain's voice. "Coop, aloft with you. See if that sail is out there yet. Take the second's glass, and don't come down until eight bells."

"Aye, sir, eight bells."

"Mr. Duncan, all working sails."

"Yes, sir. Full sail."

"And only the spanker on the mizzen. Chips has repairs to make to that top mast."

"Yes, sir."

"I smell grub. First watch will break fast after the sails are set. Helmsman, your course?"

"Southeast, sir."

CHAPTER 7

THERE'S NO SIGN of the ship that was sighted at dusk. Was it a navy ship that didn't give chase? Or another merchant or whaler that fled from *Atalanta*? Regardless, Coop gets his extra ration of grog and works the rest of his watch half drunk. He is the crew's favorite watchman now. The men have a new affection for their ship as well. As they go about their chores, basking in sunshine, last night's storm is already almost forgotten.

"That was nothin', Doc," Spanky vows as Sam splints his arm.

"How can you say that?" Sam asks. "I don't think your arm would agree."

"This? Why, it'll be good as new." Spanky looks up, eyes wide. "Will it not?"

"It will if you don't go aloft for a fortnight. The mizzen top didn't fare so well, though."

"Listen to you, eh? You sound like a regular jack tar. But it wasn't *Atalanta*'s fault. We didn't strike her sails soon enough. No, she stood well and fast and told us where her weakness was."

"You make it sound like she's alive."

Spanky's tone turns serious. "My blood! She *is* alive! Don't think for a minute that she isn't. She's alive as you and me, I swear it." Sam doesn't know what to say, so Spanky goes on, "Don't make her mad, Doc. Talk to her. Thank her for your life. Promise me."

"You're serious!"

"I am! She's all that stands between us and Davy Jones. Take care of her like yer takin' care of my arm here, and she'll take care of us.

The Horn won't come up on us so sudden. We'll have the royals and t'gallants down on deck, and she'll be ready for it. But now? Now we might put in somewhere for repairs, and you know what that means."

"No, what's it mean?"

"Goin' ashore? Women, man. Wait until you see 'em. They can't wait for us."

"Oh, I'm sure they can't." Sam means to sound sarcastic but is taken aback by his own imagining.

"That squall did us a favor, it did. And the Brits what took our spare timber. To repair the mizzen top, we will put in. Otherwise, we'd have been stuck out here until the Pacific."

"Is it mermaids we'll find there?"

"Oh no, Doc. There's islands there. The Sandwich Islands and Tahiti and, Christ, South Pacific women! They're the best of all. The smoothest skin you'll ever touch, the color of caramel, eyes of fire, and women there don't wear no shirts. Picture that! They don't need 'em. And they don't need shame neither." Spanky licks his lips. "They know you're lookin' when you can't stop starin', and they laugh about it. Like they like it too. Which they do. I don't know who's got who when I get aholt of one of them. One time, I was starin' at three of 'em and walked smack into a tree. Nearly knocked myself out. Flat on the ground, I was. Next thing I knew, I opened my eyes with my head in one of their laps. Them smilin' and gigglin'. They played with me like a toy. Happiest day of my life. I started lookin' for trees to run into."

Sam laughs. Until Spanky's story, he'd been too tired to remember the pleasures he shared with his wife. He feels an ache overtake him and wonders what these women might be like. Uncomfortable, he changes the subject. "Will it blow that hard around the Horn?"

"Oh, half again more and for weeks on end, not hours."

"What?"

"It's not the wind to worry about, though. It's the waves. Waves that run around the bottom of the world forever, never stoppin' and always growin'. Waves as tall as the masts."

"That can't be true!"

"I wish it weren't."

"No ship could survive that."

"Not to mention the bone achin' cold," Spanky goes on, "and never-endin' rain. Which can freeze. If the rigging ices up, we're goners for sure. We go aloft to chip it off, and some of us will fall."

"Spanky, you're goin' too far. It can't be that bad." The more Sam objects, the less sure he feels.

"It can be, Doc. And has been for many a ship. There be more ships on the bottom there than anywhere. After a month or two tryin' to round the Horn, a ship will turn tail and go t'other way. Around Africa. Maybe that's why that cape is named Hope. 'Tis stormy too, but not so cold. At least it'll be summer when we get to the Horn. Hell, in the summer, there's hurricanes where we just came from, blowin' twice as hard as last night. It all depends on the weather."

"I guess it always has," Sam admits, "on the farm too."

❊ ❊ ❊

Eamon confirms the near future for Sam. At the captain's desk, he finds a hand-drawn chart of a place named Buenos Aires in a newly independent country. With the Spanish deposed, the captain is uncertain of the politics there. So, he plans their exit at the same time he plans their approach. Eamon comes to realize that the captain feels safer at sea than on or near land.

After sighting gulls for the first time in two months, the crew is not surprised when *Atalanta* crosses a distinct line into muddy brown water. It's a sign that a river nearby empties into the ocean. The following dawn, the call comes down from the rigging. "Land ho!" Only the helmsman stays in place while the rest of the crew hastens to the rail or climbs the rigging to glimpse the shore. They slap each other's backs in anticipation. The captain calls all hands.

"Stand by! If I'm alarmed by anything on our approach, we will reverse course. Otherwise, this will be a brief stop to replace the mizzen topmast and careen if there's a beach to do a proper job of her bottom. We don't want to limp around the Horn. You will work from the dawn to the dog watch. The first watch will have wages and shore leave after the first day's work; the second will have the next night's leave. We should get underway after two days. Anyone late for work will forfeit his leave. Anyone late for shoving off will be collected and bear a dozen lashes. Is this clear?" It is not a question. "Mates! Start your watches to make ready."

The captain increasingly checks landmarks. A crewman at the fore-chains of the ship calls out the depth when the lead line finds bottom. Eamon makes notes as directed. An anchor is hung from its cathead. Two longboats are lowered and towed astern in case the wind dies and the crew must row to pull *Atalanta* into the anchorage. One by one, the sails are furled. The wind holds enough for her to make way and join the other half-dozen ships at anchor.

Canoes and skiffs set out from shore to meet *Atalanta*. They are a floating market. In addition to fruits, vegetables, and meat for sale, there are souvenirs of feathers, wood, silver, exotic birds, and small monkeys. Two crewmen are armed with muskets and instructed to repel anyone attempting to board. They stare the vendors down until one boat arrives full of women smiling, waving, and calling out, "Lupita's! Lupita's!" *Atalanta*'s crew cheers. When another boatload of women arrives shouting the name of another brothel, the first tries to stay between them and *Atalanta*. A proper water fight breaks out, and the men go wild.

It is dark by the time the captain is rowed off to another ship at anchor. On the foredeck, men sing and dance to a fiddle and drum. As the music dies, few of them sleep. Those that do lie on sails on deck, where the air is fresh and they can see the shore whenever they stir. The rest gather in small groups, trading impressions and stoking each other's hopes for what they'll find on their leave.

Sam stands beside Eamon, staring at the distant jungle under the moon's silver light. "It's been too long since I smelled land."

"Do the goats and chickens smell it too, Sam? They seem restless."

"They are. Lord, it smells good! All of it, even what stinks. I must've been afraid I'd never see land again, that it might have all vanished."

"I never appreciated green like this," Eamon adds, "and the bright colors of those birds. I wished dark wouldn't fall."

"The fires and torches are a sight too. Did you see where the captain's gig went?"

"He said something about mail and getting more local knowledge from one of the other ships. He didn't want to wait for the harbormaster in the morning."

"I can't wait to feel ground under my feet. And those women! Somethin' in my teeth ached to see 'em."

"I couldn't stop watching either, but I don't plan to visit them. This is my chance, Sam. One of these ships may be northbound."

Sam's eyes grow big. He looks around to see that no one is close by and lowers his voice. "Eamon! You heard the old man. He doesn't intend to lose what little crew he has. You'd be riskin' your hide."

"I've got no choice, Sam. I've got to get back. How long can Rebecca carry on? And Alex and Amy are so young. What will happen to them?"

"My Maggie is stout enough, and she's got three sons and a daughter to help. But you. If you get caught, they say the cat-o'nine-tails can kill a man."

"The captain won't kill me when he needs the few men he's got."

"But he might steal more men here."

"Sam, I'm not arguing with you, but if I tried to stop myself, I couldn't. I've got to get back. If I don't, I might as well die."

"How would you go about it"—Sam pauses—"and how can I help?"

Eamon didn't expect that. "Sam? You don't need to get in trouble. I was thinking aloud and shouldn't have said anything. All I can ask is that you keep this to yourself."

"No, I don't need trouble, but, as you said, we're not arguing. You can't stop yourself trying, and you can't stop me helpin'. What's your plan?"

"I'm only now comin' up with one. It's gonna take talking to the other crews to find a ship, but that will take you away from time with a woman."

"Don't worry. I bet the women will know more than the men anyway."

"At the least, I can steal some of the captain's paper and ink to get a letter to Becca. If you write to Maggie, I'll send it too."

"Would you do that? I'd be grateful, but"—Sam looks out to shore and then down, his tone changing—"but Maggie can't read, and I . . . I can't write so good."

"If you tell me what you want to say, I'll write it for you the best I can, and Rebecca will read it to her."

"That'd be grand, it would." Sam pauses again. "But what will I say? I've never talked a lot."

"Don't worry, Sam. I think she'll remember that."

Ashore, Eamon's sea legs are a liability, and, at first, he stumbles. *As if the ground is moving under my feet!* he thinks.

It turns out that two of the ships at anchor are British, one of them a navy frigate. The other four are Dutch, Portuguese, French, and American. The American is a whaler outbound, going the wrong direction for Eamon's purpose. Only the frigate and Portuguese are northbound, but Eamon is leery of being pressed into her majesty's navy, and he speaks no Portuguese. The bosun on the frigate assures him that "of course" his letters will be handed from ship to ship to miraculously arrive in Marblehead. Eamon shakes his head that random chance drives an age-old postal system subject to shipwrecks.

He spends the night going from tavern to inn to brothel to pub in search of a way home, but home is so far away. He doesn't speak the local language, knows no one, and has almost no money to buy the help he will need. *Can I hide here and wait for a ship that may not arrive? How long could I wait?* At last, he lays his head down on a corner table in a now quiet cantina and falls asleep. Paddy and Will'm are harsh when they "collect" him in the morning.

CHAPTER 8

15 **OF DECEMBER**, *Year of our Lord, 1810*
Buenos Aires, South America
My Dearest Becca,

I am aggrieved beyond telling. I did not understand how much I love you until now. Alex and Amy, as well. I apologize that I did not appreciate you all as much as you deserve. May Providence and my own will return me to you, I will know better. My tears of grief will turn to gratitude and joy.

No doubt you have realized that I am shanghaied, along with Sam Holbrook and the cooper's son. There were two others taken. One himself a sailor. The other never awoke. Dead, he was cast overboard. I do not know who he was; perhaps you have heard of someone gone missing.

If this letter reaches you, keep it safe. It bears witness against the captain if ever he returns to Marblehead. I am, as well, writing a letter on Sam's behalf. He will bid what he would have me write. Please convey it to Maggie.

The name of this ship is Atalanta. The captain's name is Rolinson. Her homeport was Baltimore, but she's been sold to a company in Hong Kong. The last I remember was finishing a final pint in the King's Rook. I don't know if Adam and Molly put something in our beer, or maybe we were knocked on the head. At the least, do not trust them, and if you share my suspicion, be discreet. I have no memory of a fight, though. So, there is naught to forget. This makes no sense, does it?

I would say you cannot imagine my feelings, but then neither can I of what you feel at my sudden absence. Please know that as I live and breathe, I will never stop trying to return to you. Until then, engage some help, find a journeyman, do everything possible to keep body and soul together.

This is our first landfall since awaking many weeks ago. We would not have called here if our rigging had not suffered damage in a storm. I write these words knowing you cannot fathom their meaning. It was beyond my ken to picture life at sea or what the word "storm" can mean.

There are other ships at anchor here. I will endeavor to find one to deliver this letter to you and, Lord willing, me with it. Failing that, we prepare to round Cape Horn and cross the Pacific Ocean to Atalanta's new homeport.

Every time we come to shore, I will write to you, and I will do all I can to come back. My resolve is determined. I will not give up. I cannot. Please do not give up on me. Please, unless you must.

I face a crisis of faith. How is it that this has happened? How can I trust in Him? But you, dear Becca, I trust. I put my life, my hope, in your hands.

I love you, I love you, I love you, each and all three.
Your loving husband and devoted father,
Eamon.

15 of December, Year of our Lord, 1810
Buenos Aires, South America
Dear Maggie,

I am not dead! At least not yet. The night I did not come home, I was shanghaied. I'm on a ship named Atalanta. We are anchored in a harbor in South America. It is my first sight of land in so many weeks. You would not believe how much of the world has no land. How much of it is covered by water.

I am sorry I wasn't there for the harvest. I trust the boys and Elizabeth did their share and mine too. If you sell some land, it will be less to manage and will put money by for planting. Keep the woods, though, so you can sell timber. Or sell livestock, but no more than you must. Eamon McGrath is here with me. And so is young Coop. There's a sailor named Jack with us too. Another poor fellow died that night, and they dropped him overboard.

They call me 'Doc' here, after I patched up Eamon from his fight with the first mate. I take care of men now instead of horses and cows. At least there are some chickens here and two goats, and there was a pig until we butchered her.

Eamon is writing this out for me. He says Rebecca will read it to you if it reaches you. I don't know if it will. I miss you and the boys and Elizabeth and the farm. Remember me, please. Tell Ben he's the man of the house now, and bid the others to listen to him (after he listens to you). Please give Rebecca what help you can.

I hope the best for you. Lord willing, I will come home soon.

Your mule,
Sam

Rebecca looks up from the page at Maggie. They sit across from each other on bench seats at the long oak table that is the center of Maggie's house. An unlit whale-oil lamp hangs above. The front door behind Becca is open. Bright spring sunshine pours in and warms the fir floor to the color of honey. To each side of the door, an open window is deep set in thick log walls. Crisp air ruffles plain, coarse curtains. Between the door and the window to its right, various sized coats hang from hooks. There's a bench below the window, and leather boots are tucked under it. Below the window to the left, a sink is in the middle of a long kitchen countertop of thick pine. Shelves hold containers and staples, a copper pitcher, dishes, mugs, table linens, and a sectioned box of cutlery. A wooden bucket sits below the sink. Pots and pans hang from a rafter. A rack, covered with herbs and plants to dry, is raised to the ceiling by string and pulleys.

A stone hearth is centered on the wall behind Maggie. Steam rises from a blackened pot hanging above a small fire. Two stout chairs face the hearth, one a rocking chair, each with a needle-point cushion on its seat. A small table stands between them. To both sides of the hearth is a closed door, and next to each is a ladder that leads up to a sleeping loft. Everything is worn but clean and in its place. There is an economy about the space.

The two women smile, awkward as their teary eyes meet.

"It's an old joke between us." Maggie wipes her eyes with the apron she wears. "He works so hard and is so stubborn, I tell him his name should be mule Sam instead of Samuel." She looks down and back up. "And they call him 'Doc' now. After patchin' up Eamon from a fight? That doesn't sound like Eamon, does it?"

"Not at all. Maggie, these letters are more than three months old. Why didn't Eamon and Sam come themselves? What happened? Where are they?"

"If they're even alive." Maggie shakes her head. "Oh, Rebecca, forgive me. I don't mean to make it worse." She pauses. "He'd be proud of you and Alex and Amy getting on so well."

"And of you and so many neighbors. You've all been good to us. I can hardly buy our food. We'd not have survived winter without your help."

"We were blessed with a bounty, and you helped with putting it away."

"To be certain, I cannot take food from your table without repaying what I can. I'll not forget your generosity."

"I'd not want to hear Minister's sermon if we failed you. And we're beholden for you startin' a few of us learnin' our letters."

"I hope to do more. As long as I still have the shop, I can get signs up along the road to Boston, for our market."

"So, you're not goin' to sell it?"

"The print shop? No, not so far. 'Tis all we have, and we'd not get a fair price." Rebecca looks down. "It's my luck Eamon let me help him, that I learned enough to carry on. I'm drumming up business in Swampscott and Lynn and paying Zachary Silvers to deliver. As the days grow longer, he's able to go farther. And I'm considering starting a weekly news."

"Amy says Mister Anderson orders the bank's printing from you."

"Yes, more than he needs, really." Rebecca pauses, tired, but brightens. "Timothy's help has been a gift. Thank you for it."

"He's a hard worker. Always has been. And he has a hunger for books, when I can spare him. I think he would work for free if you keep lettin' him into your library."

"Oh no, he deserves to be paid. Alex helps too, of course, after school. Oh, Maggie!" Rebecca wilts. "He's alive. I mean, they are. Or at least they were." Each breath comes shallower until she bursts. "Dear Lord, forgive me, but curse these letters! They leave me, I mean, us, caught. Caught between hopeless and hopeful."

"Were we not anyway?"

"And look at my hands! How did he keep ink from getting on everything? My clothes are a mess despite his apron. This is the only dress I haven't ruined. I save it for church and whenever I leave the house. What would he think?"

"Like I said, he'd be proud. He always was. We all saw that. The Lord blessed you both with love."

Rebecca shakes her head. "What happened then? Did we sin? Do we deserve this punishment? And if so, how long before He sees us fit for debtor's prison?"

"Now, now, we'll not be lettin' that happen to you."

"Thank you, truly. I trust your help, but it's Mister Anderson and the baker, I suspect. They're too kind, and I am pained they are widowers. Can they not tell I'll not marry them, that I don't love them? I'm still married to Eamon, and he's not gone a year yet."

"Ah, Rebecca, you're too pretty. They can't help themselves."

"Pretty? Look at me! And my hair."

"They know better. They've seen your smile and heard your laugh."

"Not lately, they haven't."

"I mean they remember it, when Eamon was here."

"Well, they needn't remember. That was then, and this, this is different. *I* am different. Anymore, I'm not who they saw or heard."

"I know, dear. It's hard to imagine anything but trouble from this. At least we're better friends, though, almost a big family."

"I apologize, but I would rather have him back, friends or no."

"Of course, you would, but that choice isn't ours, and we'll make the best we can of it. This is a hard time for sure and certain, but the good Lord wouldn't give it to us if we weren't able for it."

Rebecca tilts her head and looks back at the older woman. "You're stronger than I am, Maggie, or wise beyond me."

"I don't know about bein' wise. Farmers face a lot of things we cannot control. So, we come to terms with whatever we must, and cry sometimes too. To smile and laugh, despite a life gone mad, can feel like revenge."

"Mad? I soon will be."

"Oh no, you won't. In fact, I think these letters call for a celebration. Send Amy over to help with the cookin', and join us for dinner. We'll all toast that if these letters can get through to us, so can our men."

At last, Rebecca drops her face into her hands. The older woman pushes her bench back, stands, comes around the table, and rests her hands on Becca's shaking shoulders.

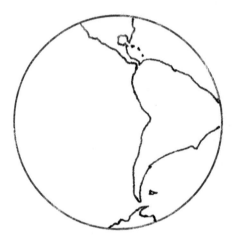

CHAPTER 9

"EAMON, YOU CAN'T stay up here," Coop coaxes, but Eamon's eyes remain shut tight. "You missed supper, but Cook set something aside for you."

His first time ordered aloft, Eamon clings to the main topgallant mast. Each time he dares open his eyes, his fear slams them shut. He holds on tighter and hears whispers between sailcloth and wind, creaking in the rigging and, far below, the whoosh of water. *Atalanta*'s motion is amplified on high. His stomach churns, and bile rises in his throat.

"Not much of a lookout," he chokes out, "if I can't open my eyes."

"Don't worry. You made it to the end of your watch, but you've got to come down now."

"Right. I'm coming," he says but doesn't move.

"You don't want Mister Duncan sending someone else up to get you down. Or worse, come for you himself."

With this new fear, Eamon's eyes open. "When did it get dark?"

"Not long ago. Maybe it's easier if you can't see."

"Maybe." He tries to take a deep breath and forces himself to look around. "How far up am I?"

"A hundred feet, easy. Taller than most trees, and you're still below the masthead. I've even shimmied up the lifts, squeezed past the spider band, and sat atop the royal mast with nothing but my legs wrapped around it to hold on."

"But this tree is moving!"

"Only a little. You're lucky it's calm, your first time aloft. You can feel every ripple up here, like they're inside you. The wind and sails talk to me, and at the masthead, I feel like I'm flying. I look down at birds that go by, and the ship looks so small from here. On a clear night, when I look up, the stars are endless. If it's flat calm, they're on the water, too, and we drift upon them. Eamon, I never knew there was anything like this. It only happens up here. Where I'm alone and there's nothing between me . . ." Coop pauses when he feels Eamon's gaze. "Me and God. Do I sound crazy?"

"Not at all, Coop. You sound like a poet."

"Really?"

"Yeah, but that's beside the point, isn't it?" Eamon hears the tension in his own voice. "I mean, you're right, I really must get down. And soon."

"Yes, you must."

"How am I going to do that? I can't seem to let go. You might have to pry my fingers loose."

"I can do that. Just don't look down." Coop sets to work loosening Eamon's grip. "Don't look at anything but the ratline you're grabbing. I'll be below you and guide your feet as we go. So, don't look down. Right?"

"Right." Eamon nods a little.

"Here we go, then. Come on now."

The muscles in Eamon's arms and legs cramp and uncramp and cramp again. By the time he stands on deck, he shakes from fatigue instead of fear. He feels like a puddle and sits down, his back against the bulwark. "Thank you, Coop. I'm sorry to put you through that."

"Don't worry. By the time we get to the Sandwich Islands, you'll be used to it."

Jack walks up. "Welcome back, Eamon. While you were up there, I offered odds on when you might come down. Made a little money. Seems you should 'ave some of it."

True to Coop's kind words, Eamon adjusts to climbing the rigging. He muses whether the kid waxing poetic helped. He was right; it is stunning on high. Far from the harsh reality on deck, Eamon, too, could not have imagined this. Aloft, something profound within him shifts. Since awaking aboard, he has been embittered. Now he doesn't recognize what he feels. Then he tries to deny it. The moment he beholds the beauty before him, his grip on the betrayal he suffers loosens. Of a sudden, he owns a little of this experience that wholly owns him. He hates that *Atalanta* carries him farther from home. Away from love. Away from hope. He is new to hatred so fierce: all anger and sharp, aching, relentless pain. Its intensity hollows him out. It stretches him to more than pain. It excavates a vastness inside him into which something must rush. Atop the mast, what rushes in is beauty.

Confused, he is breathless as all his senses witness the scene before him: *Atalanta's* power as she shoulders through waves, her sway to the wind, the whoosh and hiss of her wake, the wind in his hair, on his face, its voice in the sails, the groan of a shroud, the taste and smell of salt air, warm sun on skin, diamonds of sunlight dancing on the water, and an impossible depth of blue when he looks down. This sum is beyond believing and changes him. Seeing it forces him to surrender. Here is beauty, unconditional and animate: pouring in through his eyes, soaking into his skin, not waiting for witness but reaching for him, enveloping him, carrying him beyond his fortressed self. Beauty belongs to him, and he is clearly part of it. Infinitesimally small but part. This moment will be indelible to him.

He no longer knows where he belongs. He wills himself to look away, to not know that he can never return to who he was. At the masthead, Eamon is shocked to hear his own voice and the words, "Thank you." His vision blurs with tears. "No! I can't mean that." It is terrible beauty, painful joy, grief and relief, irony's sharp slap. His spirit begs for nourishment even if he does not. With each breath, air feels new. At last, he is able to accept his path. So, it is not the brutality on deck that breaks Eamon, breaks him open and compels him onward. It is beauty that breaks him.

CHAPTER 10

EVEN IN THE southern hemisphere's summer, rounding Cape Horn can take a month or more. In preparation, the topgallants and everything above them—masts, yards, rigging, and sails—are struck and stowed on deck. This far south, it is always cold. Sunlight dies on steel gray seas grown monstrous. Rain can turn to hail or snow. Shoulders hunched against the cold, the man lashed to the helm feels "frozen in place." Ropes grow stiff and the crew stiff with them. Their hands crack open, bleed, and refuse to heal. True to Spanky's augury, one of three new men from Buenos Aires falls from the rigging. In big winds and seas, there is no going back for him. He'll freeze and sink before they could reach him anyway. While it's dangerous aloft, giant waves often sweep the ship's waist. Men caught there disappear beneath them and can be swept over the side.

Coop comes down from his turn aloft and swears he looked *up* to the wavetops from the crosstrees. Eamon concurs from the end of a yardarm, where he most often finds himself when Mister Duncan orders a sail change and men aloft. When the Flemish horse breaks from under Eamon's feet, he holds on to the yardarm and slides his way back toward the mast to stand on a footrope. He looks down to see the mate watching and wonders if someone cut the "horse" nearly through.

Winds that roar at the crests of the big waves grow confused in their troughs. There, *Atalanta* stands up and slows. From the helm, Sam swears the next wave is about to bury the ship. He reminds himself that she has always risen, that every time water covers her, she sheds it. On the wavetops, the wind shrieks in the rigging again. *Atalanta* heels hard over like a toy pushed on its edge. Her speed struggles to catch up with the force in her sails. Squinting, Sam imagines his brief view is that of a mountaineer looking out over a range of peaks, but these "peaks" are moving. Then he's back in a "valley" looking up at the next wall of water charging toward him.

Square-rigged ships are fast when they sail downwind. To go upwind, they claw their way across it, just hanging on to hard-won progress. When sailors feel like they may never get where they're going, they define "destination" as *a place from which the wind blows*. When the wind turns and favors her, *Atalanta* races north and clears Cape Horn at last. Bone-cold for weeks, the crew can't reach warmer climates soon enough. Over two months, they have sailed more than three thousand nautical miles to arrive seven hundred overland miles from Buenos Aires. While trekking over the Andes is impossible, rounding the Horn is no less of a climb.

Their first day to lick their wounds is at anchor before a Spanish village built on a crescent of rocky beach and surrounded by steep, lush hillsides: Valparaiso.

"The first watch will go with Cook for water and provisions," the captain assigns. "The second will load seal skins. The sooner you're done, the sooner you'll have your leave. Eamon shall stand anchor watch, with Cook and Mister Gates. Be back tomorrow by the forenoon to weigh anchor. Don't be late."

Sam eyes Eamon. "If you can't go ashore, at least I'll not be patchin' you up again."

"The memory makes my back itch, it does. Still, I would try to jump ship, and the old man knows it. So, Sam, will you take our letters again, to send home?"

"We have letters?"

"I do. Not that it will get home, but I'll be glad to write another for you if you want."

"Certainly!"

Eamon's duties as anchor watch are to alert the captain if *Atalanta*'s anchor drags, watch that neighboring ships stay in place, and repel anyone other than crew coming aboard. If the captain disembarks and Mr. Duncan remains, Eamon seeks out the few others who are aboard as witness against the chief mate killing him and reporting that he must have escaped.

The next afternoon, Coop shows Eamon a tattoo on his left shoulder. "What do you think?"

Eamon tilts his head. "A turtle?"

"A shellback, since I am one. It was that or a full-rigged ship to show that I've sailed 'round the Horn."

"What are some others?"

"A rope around the wrist shows I'm a deckhand. There were mermaids, too, and I'll want a dolphin somewhere."

"It's handsome, Coop. Did it hurt?"

"Not much."

"Maybe Sam should look at it to make sure it doesn't turn foul?"

"It could do that?"

"At least wash it, eh?"

"But I don't want to wash it off."

"Don't worry. I don't think you can. Ask the rest of the crew."

Ten days later, *Atalanta* calls on a larger Spanish city: Callao. This part of the coast is semi-arid and brown. Eamon is again confined to the ship. Here, the captain adds coca, alpaca wool, and salt to the cargo. He has a small purchase of silver locked in his quarters.

When the men have shore leave, Sam delivers his and Eamon's letters to the harbormaster for any eastbound ship. Not far behind him, the first mate steps in to collect westbound mail and looks through the eastbound for anything addressed to *Atalanta*. When he sees two crisp envelopes addressed to Marblehead, he is suspicious and pockets them.

10 of March, Year of our Lord, 1811
Callao, South America
Dearest Becca, Alex, and Amy,

I am held captive on board again, else I would escape to bring this letter to you myself. As it is, please may it sustain you until I return.

This is a larger Spanish port, dry and hot at last. The cold from rounding the Horn was bone deep. Only now do I <u>not</u> shiver at the memory of it. The wind and waves here are more like what you witness from home. How I dream of that shore! And of you.

Two more men signed on here as crew. I cannot imagine anyone volunteering for a sailor's slavery. So, I wonder who or what they are running from.

Not knowing how you fare, I fear for you all. Was the winter harsh? Is it summer or fall by the time you read this? What comfort or succor can you find? I assure myself that you are not abandoned to desperation. I console myself, and may it console you, that I trust your strength and abilities, that our community will twin your generosity with their own, and . . .

"Well done." Captain Rolinson looks aside from the letter and then up to the mate. "We can't have him writing home like this."

"And to what use," the mate adds, "when he won't make it home anyway?"

"Your orders stand, Mister Duncan. Unless or until I change them, you will continue to distance yourself from him. Is that clear?"

"Aye, sir."

"Meanwhile, instruct the bosun and Mister Strom to watch for these letters whenever we come ashore."

❄ ❄ ❄

Sure enough, Coop returns from shore and shows Eamon the circled pattern of a compass on his right shoulder. "A compass rose! You can be proud of that one. I almost wish it were mine."

"Thank you. It's a pity you can't get one. It must be terrible, bein' kept from goin' ashore when it's so close."

"Don't worry. Maybe it helps if I *am* out of my mind."

In the month it takes to sail north to Mexico, *Atalanta* stops in the Galapagos Islands. Here, her crew hauls aboard a great tortoise. The behemoth lives long on scant food and serves as a storehouse of fresh protein when butchered.

During the line crossing, Coop lords it over the pollywogs from South America. As a merman, Eamon doesn't add coconut shells to his costume. He goes easy on the newcomers and has a good laugh at Sam's portrayal of a mermaid.

Atalanta finds revolutionary tensions in Acapulco. After a drought, and despite the 1809 food riot, the Spanish viceroyalty in Mexico City has been stealing poor harvests for itself. The peasants are hungry. The only goods they want to buy are weapons and ammunition. It is the same in Puerto Vallarta. Though unable to reprovision and sell goods, the captain can buy cochineal, tobacco, cocoa, and weavings. What he spends gives the Mexicans money they will need for their fight. These are hot and humid stops, and the sailors recall the cold of Cape Horn almost wistfully.

Sailing up the west coast of North America, at the New Spain missions of San Diego, Monterey, and San Francisco, *Atalanta* loads tanned buffalo hides: large, heavy, stiff slabs. Continuing north, the Oregon Country coastline is lonely, rugged, and dark green. When the captain goes aloft and judges the Columbia River bar too violent to cross, *Atalanta* bypasses Astoria. The farther she goes north, the more the mountain ranges march from the background to the coastline, snowcapped even in summer. In Esquimalt, the crew adds plush otter pelts to her cargo.

Sam returns from shore and looks for Eamon. "Am I back early, or is this day so long?"

"No, Sam, you're not early. We're close to the solstice and just struck four bells. Is that a British flag above that fort on shore?"

"There's a company from England here, trying to take hold. It's an outpost, really, no brothel or pub, and they're careful around the natives. If you can borrow Mr. Strom's spyglass, look at those tall poles in the village. They carve animals and faces into them."

"A proud people with a strong culture and time for art, they could worry an outpost. I was surprised no canoes came out to beg or barter."

"No, they don't need us, and they've got plenty to eat. Here, taste this."

"Oh my!" Eamon hums his appreciation. "What is it?"

"Dried salmon. From those racks along the beach. They go whaling, too, and have the bones to prove it, big things."

"It may not be as remote here as you think, Sam. We're closer to home than we've been anywhere else. Remember the expedition President Jefferson sent west? They were lucky to make it here and were gone over two years before they made it back."

"So, we're closer, but the distance is hopeless?"

"I'm afraid so. If it's an English camp, though, maybe someone has a book to sell. I'm desperate for something to read, but it would have been in Spanish before this. I haven't been able to spend my wages and ought to be able to buy a book or two."

"I'll ask when I go back tomorrow." Sam licks his fingers. "This place is so green, I can taste it in the air. I've never seen a forest so dense. It must be good soil and a good climate. Those trees, so tall and straight, look like perfect masts."

"Sam, you sound like a sailor and a farmer both."

CHAPTER 11

IT TAKES FOUR and twenty days for *Atalanta* to sail south and then ride the trade winds to the Sandwich Islands. She anchors off of Honolulu to load heavy casks of whale oil. When Sam returns from shore, he hands two books to Eamon.

"Thank you. What do I owe you?"

"Nothin'. The book seller thought your one book was worth these two."

"It *was* good, but I can read even a good book too many times. And you dropped our letters off?"

"Aye."

Eamon looks to shore. "This place looks more beautiful than any we've seen."

"It's even better up close. If I can guess what a plant is, it's triple the size of its cousins. Anything in the ground must produce more and faster. The weeds too. By the time you weed to one end of a field, you would need to go back to fight 'em off at the other end. You wouldn't need a big field, though. A man could work half as hard and harvest twice as much, year-round."

"Would you stay if you could?"

"Who wouldn't? Once you get away from the wharves and filth and into the hills, the thought's hard to resist."

"Especially with a Polynesian beauty as your guide, Sam?"

"That too. Didn't want to bring it up, with you trapped on board."

"Coop told me about her. To be honest, I can't take my eyes off the women, either, but I'm not sure how I'd be with anyone other than Becca."

"I think about my Maggie, too, but Pualani makes it too easy. Her and the whiskey her family makes. Them bein' farmers, we talk the same language even without the same words."

"Would they hide you until we sail?"

"It's not that simple, Eamon. This island isn't the place I know, and neither are these people. We're worlds apart. Pualani's not one of the whores in town, but just the same, they take my money. Whose money do they take when we sail? Eamon, I'm not sure I belong anywhere—not at sea and not on shore. Where does that leave me?"

"Oh, for God's sake, Sam, jump ship if you can. From the decks of hell, you're lookin' heaven in the eye."

"But they've seen the likes of me and Captain Rolinson before. Even if I tried to stay, they'd know which ship is mine and where to ask what I'm worth. It wouldn't cost the old man much to make sure I sober up back on board. I'm not blaming them; it's not their fault. They were better off before these ships came calling. Now they carry on despite us. It's ugly in town, and they'd as soon keep us cornered there. When I wandered into the hills, a couple natives with machetes sent me back until Pualani spoke for me."

"Sounds to me like they *should* be hostile."

"Besides, Eamon, if I jumped ship, who'd help you get home?"

"Ha! Or die trying, Sam?"

"You might have if I hadn't patched you up. Twice now. And suppose you make it. What would they think if I stayed here?"

"Who? Our families? Don't worry, Sam. Who could blame you? Besides, if you've noticed, we're only getting farther from home."

"What if you make it, though? I'm not gonna leave my story for you to tell."

Eamon tilts his head, narrows his eyes, and lowers his voice. "What are you sayin', Sam?"

"Sure, I want off this ship, but not just off. If you can make it home, I can too."

"Oh, Sam, be careful now. I'm telling you, I don't know if I *can* make it. And if it goes wrong, it's only *my* hide. Besides, I can move faster alone. Even if it *is* God's will that I make it back, that doesn't mean home is waiting for me. It's changing all the time. I can't stop thinking about it. I've pictured walking through the door of my shop a thousand times, but it might not be mine anymore. I can see myself going up the steps, but I can't picture if Rebecca would wrap her arms around me or not. I couldn't blame her, y'know. What has it been, a year? And if I get back, two or three. In truth, I'm fearful of what I'll find if I make it, but I'll go through hell to get there."

"If this is hell, Eamon, what have we got to lose? Here we are, tearin' around the world as if we're goin' somewhere, and we're not. It's always another place we don't belong, another place we leave behind. More than my crops, maybe I need roots. I've got to stop someplace to put 'em down, and home's my best chance, even if it's changed."

Eamon slaps *Atalanta*'s wood railing, turns, and takes a few steps away.

Sam's voice falls on his back. "What do you say?"

When he wipes his eyes and turns back, Eamon shakes his head. "Sam, what *can* I say? I'll not tell you what to do, but do we even have a chance? It's one thing to get myself killed. What if you die tryin'?"

"Does it matter? It's a miracle the mate hasn't killed you yet. If you've survived this long, anything is possible. Once you're on the move, you'll still need someone at your back. Little guy like you could use a man my size."

"You'll not be easy to hide in a crowd, and what about me at your back? You could use someone bigger."

"Who might you suggest?" Sam reaches out to shake on their partnership.

Eamon stares at Sam's hand. "Before I shake your hand, I've got to make one thing clear. I'll listen to you, but this will not be a democracy. What I say goes. I call the shots, and you can stand down any time you want, but if you haven't backed out, I'll not go without you. I promise that."

"You call the shots," Sam consents, his hand still extended, "and I'll keep patchin' you up."

Eamon grabs Sam's hand and shakes it. Hard.

CHAPTER 12

MIDDAY WEEKS LATER, *Atalanta*'s bow wave is a steady rumble as warm wind bears her west. Everyone is on deck, at the helm or at a chore. When a ship full of misfits is at sea for months, tensions build. Horny and half drunk on rations of grog, little more than convicts, some men spoil for a fight. So, a ship's regimen leaves the crew little time to know their own pulse. Landlubbers ask if sailors get bored at sea, and sailors always answer no. Beyond the spell the sea casts, there is always hard work at hand. A captain needs to keep his crew busy. If weather turns calm, seeming to let the next landfall recede, he orders marlinspike work done and redone.

Sam enjoys the ropework and thinks it will serve him well on the farm. Busy with rope, twine, and marlinspike, he hears Toren's voice call down from the rigging, "Ahoy, below, off to starboard, dolphins coming to us." He pauses to look up from the sunny patch of deck where he works. "Bloody," he hears from aloft, "thousands of 'em!" Sam gets to his feet and the side of the ship.

No matter how many times a sailor sees dolphins, his heart bounds out to meet them. Four dolphins fly abreast of each other straight out from the face of a wave. They jockey what looks too fast and too close under the bow. Some turn on their sides and, you would swear, look you in the eye. When one flips in midair, it can only be for fun. You'd think they swim hard to keep up. But no. On moonless nights, wrapped in bioluminescence, their bright-green cloaks reveal that they are loafing to pace the ship with ease. Sharks, hated by all sailors, depart whenever dolphins arrive. Sailors take them for a good omen. No matter how threatening a storm may be, men in need of hope find comfort when dolphins are nearby. Myth has it that dolphins are sailors lost at sea, reincarnated. If this be so, being lost at sea doesn't look so bad.

Coop is aloft up the foremast, brushing the rigging with hot pine tar from a pail. He looks out from his perch and sees dorsal fins strafing through the water across the horizon, heading south. "Look at 'em all."

Scraping the windlass for a fresh coat of paint, Eamon is in the perfect place to watch the dolphins carving *Atalanta*'s bow wave. He lays his tools down, looks over the bow from side to side, and climbs out on the bowsprit to watch them.

When Jack and a few others go forward, Eamon shouts to them, "Where are they coming from and where bound? Famine must follow in their wake."

"There's not a lot of food in the middle of the ocean," Jack answers. "At least, we haven't caught any lately."

"Maybe there's food down deep. This is only the surface."

"Oh, no!" Coops voice comes down from the rigging. "WATCH OUT!"

It's too late. Will'm, en route to the bow, looks up and can dodge the falling pail but not the hot tar. It splashes his face, shoulders, and bare chest. He screams and can't stop trying to wipe it off, but that makes it worse. "Bloody hell, get it off me!" He drops to his knees.

Coop is somehow down on deck and beside the stricken man before anyone else can reach him. Horrified, he begs, "What do I do?"

"Douse him! Douse him with water," calls Chips. "Cool him off." Two or three buckets of water are snatched from alongside *Atalanta* and splashed on Will'm. His writhing slows, his howls soften to whimpers, and he lies still.

More of the crew gather. Eamon, too. Rye bursts into their midst. "Balls!" He jumps at Coop. "You're flamin' dangerous!" Coop doesn't fight back. Someone pulls Rye back. More men join the fray. Sam tries to push them away from Will'm's inert form and gets punched for his trouble. He stumbles back and then grabs Will'm by the ankles to pull him clear. Eamon finds himself facing the chief mate. He backs up but bumps into someone who holds him tight. A shot rings out. Wood splinters from the foremast above the men's heads. Still, Mister Duncan deals Eamon a blow, and Eamon drops. The men all turn to face the captain, standing at the mainmast, saber in one hand and a pistol in the other. At his side, the bosun reloads the pistol that was fired.

"Who started this?" he demands. A confusion of voices shout "Rye" while others name Coop. The captain holds up a hand. When quiet follows, he asks, "Mister Duncan?"

"It was Coop, sir."

"But it was an accident, sir," Coop objects. "It was"—his eyes meet the captain's—"my accident, sir. I dropped the tar. And Will'm was below me. I'm . . . I apologize. It was stupid. I was watching the dolphins."

"Twelve lashes at eight bells." The captain's words are final. "Now, all of you back to work, or there will be more to pay. Mister Gates, get this mess cleaned up. Doc, do what you can for him."

"Easy, men," Sam instructs as they lay Will'm out on a hatch. "I need somethin' to clean this off him. Someone see if Cook can spare a few of the captain's eggs. I've heard the whites can treat burns." When skin peels off with the tar, Sam is glad Will'm is out cold. Next, he patches a few wounds from the fight.

While Coop paces on deck to calm himself, Eamon stands before the captain's desk, holding his gut and pleading, "Sir, please, you can't mean to punish Coop for an innocent mistake."

The captain returns a pistol to its holster at the back of his chair. "You'll *not* tell me what I cannot do."

"He didn't start that fight, though, didn't even fight back when Rye jumped him."

"The fight started, did it not? And why did it start?"

"Coop was the first one at Will'm's side to help him. I'll never know how he got down so fast."

"Eamon, I will captain my crew. There are consequences to mistakes, innocent or not. Twelve lashes is a kindness. I will have every last one of you whipped if that's what it takes to keep this ship on course."

"Sir, please . . ."

"Is that clear?"

Eamon draws a breath to speak his mind but gives up. "Yes. Sir."

"Then you are dismissed." Half a heartbeat passes. "Now!"

CHAPTER 13

EAMON STANDS ON deck, numb to his surroundings. Within him is a blinding darkness toward which he dare not turn. An edge lies there, a vibration that shakes him to his bones. *Have I been here before? A nightmare, something rushing at me that I can't survive. Not again.* Glancing sideways at Coop, Eamon winces. Coop's arms are lashed to the mainmast, his back bare. He steals a glance over his shoulder at Eamon.

Between them, the deck is clear. Eamon is aware of men to either side and the officers behind him. His pulse drums in his ears. The air he breathes feels serrated. He looks down again at the sunny deck and the cat-o'nine-tails in his hand. The last strike of the ship's bell fades. Time itself feels thick and slow.

"Get on with it," Mister Duncan growls, "or take his place."

Yes, Eamon thinks. *NO!* his body answers. *But I can't do this. Not to Coop. This will tear, it will scar, but if I hold back, they'll know it.*

"Eamon"—Coop's voice is low and unsure—"get it over with. I'm ready."

No, you're not. Eamon steps closer to Coop. He looks up. The sky gives him no answer, no way out. "Forgive me," he whispers. He can delay no longer. He rears back, raises his arm, and feels the crew hold their breath. As he brings the cat down with all his might, time stretches. He hears the whips whisper and hiss through the air before they thunder on impact. Nine sharp knots claw at Coop's back, each welt appearing suddenly, some with a thin scratch of blood. Coop bites back his pain; still, a sharp grunt escapes him. Eamon mistakes it for his own. As his stroke follows through, a shock reverberates up his arm, into his veins. From that darkness inside him, a seductive evil shrieks, triumphant. A grimace contorts Eamon's face.

He rears back again but swings blindly this time and throws the hideous thing overboard. "NO!" he shouts. Then quiet. "No, I can't do it." He looks up to the captain and shrugs. Two men grab hold of him, and he almost laughs. "What's your hurry, mates? Where am I gonna go? I want to take Coop's place anyway."

Eyes fixed on Eamon, the captain's expression betrays no emotion at all. His voice is almost tired. "Lash him to the other side of the mast. Leave 'em both for the night. No food or drink. Swede, make up another cat and have it ready by dawn. We'll break it in on Coop's back and then fifty strokes on Eamon's. All hands back to your stations." He turns and goes to his cabin.

After they tie Eamon in place, he and Coop look around the mast to face each other.

"Forgive me, Coop. I couldn't help it. I should've traded with you to start, and this'd be over by now."

"You *are* crazy. Fifty lashes?"

"Believe me, I don't mean to keep Sam busy."

"It was my fault. I got you into this."

"No, you didn't. In truth, it was inevitable."

"But I dropped the tar."

"It was an accident, Coop. It could've been anyone. It happened, that's all."

"At least Sam thinks Will'm will heal."

"He may be uglier, if that's possible."

"He really is a Jack Tar now, eh?"

As condemned men can, Coop and Eamon become a little giddy. They try to keep their minds from what's to come. Through the night, their occasional chuckle surprises the crew, but Eamon baffled them from the start. They never imagined anyone volunteering to be beaten. He started to seem regular enough, a little like themselves, until now. By first light, he and Coop have fallen silent, their exhaustion obvious.

※ ※ ※

"Is he dead?" Coop rubs his wrists, now free from the mast. Still shaking, he helps Jack lay unconscious Eamon on the deck.

"No," Jack answers, "it takes time to die from a beatin.'"

Sam has buckets of seawater ready. "He's passed out and might be glad of it when I pour this over his back. It will sting, but it's the best thing. And you, too, Coop. Salt in your wounds, I'm afraid." As he pours the water, Eamon doesn't stir.

Coop can't keep quiet. "He kept looking into my eyes, right there, close. I wanted to scream for him, but his eyes shut me up, until they rolled back. Why didn't he howl like the first time?"

There is respect in Jack's answer, "'E wouldn't give the mate the satisfaction."

"I'm sure it helped you were there, Coop." Sam tries to comfort the boy. "And maybe it helps if he *is* mad. Swede, refill these buckets?"

"On my way."

"All right, young man. Bend over and brace yourself." Sam sets to work, pouring. Coop hisses a breath in.

※ ※ ※

When Eamon is back at the captain's desk days later, all dialog is gone. Theirs is a strict monologue now—the captain either dictates or has pages transcribed. Eamon's only words are "Yes, sir" and "No, sir." His questions are gone while his education continues: on deck and at the helm, with logs, inventories, manifests, and repairs, dead reckoning notes and noon sights, and updates on harbors, markets, and vendors.

Eamon's back eventually scabs over, but the scabs crack and

bleed such that he can't wear a shirt. Swede fashions a loose poncho for him, but it's not much better. Unable to sleep on his back, a hammock is not an option. On deck in the folds of a sail might be comfortable, but he's too wary of the first mate to sleep there. He ends up wedging himself into a corner of the forecastle with his arms wrapped around his duffle to cushion the night. No matter how carefully he moves, he winces. By the time he can move apace, most of his back is a mass of soft pink scars. There remains a numbness and a continual sensation of cold in his left hand. His status among the crew has somehow grown.

"'E's a survivor, 'e is."

"Can you believe it? Christ almighty, that was a beatin'."

"'E had to know it was comin' when 'e threw the cursed thing overboard."

"But he didn't know what he was doin'."

"The mate got 'is licks in, eh? But 'e is tough, not a sound from him."

"Real calm, he was. Don't know how he did it."

"He's bloody mad! That's 'ow 'e did it."

CHAPTER 14

IN THE SOUTH Pacific islands, the captain sells more cargo than he purchases. Cook adds breadfruit to the crew's diet. In Sydney, *Atalanta* swings at anchor to ship wool aboard.

The captain reports to the harbormaster and visits one of the American flagged whalers. When he returns, shore leave begins. The men row themselves ashore in two longboats. Eamon is, of course, on anchor watch again. This place is made up of convicts. While there is respectable commerce here, most of the crew is ashore patronizing the less respected kind.

Lantern light and sound drift to Eamon from shore through warm, dry night air. One boat returns, rowed by two oarsmen and helmed by the bosun. It bumps alongside. Eamon catches its painter and then a stern line. He leads them through some rigging and pins them to keep the little boat in place while his mates climb back aboard. The bosun is last up with a canvas bag over his shoulder. Not breaking his stride, he passes close by Eamon and nearly punches him in the belly. Reflexively, Eamon goes to stop the punch. The bosun lets something go into Eamon's hands and mutters, "Captain forgot the mail," whereupon he strides aft and descends the companionway. There, in Eamon's hands, are three letters.

Astonished, he manages to thrust them into a pocket before glancing around, nervous to keep his secret. In a glimpse, he recognizes Rebecca's handwriting. Too many emotions rush through him. He looks up and then out over the harbor, glances around again, and peeks into his pocket. One envelope is addressed to him, another to Sam, the third to Coop. He starts to smile as tears start down his face. *What's it been? Over a year? And this, here in my hands.* Something in his belly clenches. Now it's in his chest and then at his throat. He's not able to say a word even if he must. He pounds *Atalanta*'s rail with a fist, looks away again, wipes his face, and shakes his head.

What mail comes is almost always for the captain. There are few literate people on board who could have read the envelopes. *What luck!* Eamon thinks. *I must thank Gates. Discreetly. When did she write this? Eight months ago? Six? And how did it get here? Where has it been? Are there others? If so, where are they?* He shakes his head and looks to shore. *I better calm down. But her words are here in my pocket. What will she say?* Of a sudden, he feels afraid. *What* will *she say?*

He listens; the ship is quiet. He goes forward where the anchor light hangs from the forestay. There, he can read by the light that spills from it. He is alone. Still, he shelters the pages from anyone who might come on deck and is ready to stuff them away.

> *15 April, Year of 1811*
> *Beloved,*
>
> *I miss you terribly. But I cannot let that stop me. After all, I have two children to raise and a printing business to carry on. Yes, I've still got the business. You should see the ink on my hands. How did you keep your hands clean? It's everywhere. Even upstairs in the kitchen, on the furniture. Your apron is nearly black now.*
>
> *Of course, we knew what happened before your letters arrived. The Malloys say you left The King's Rook last they saw you.*
>
> *I showed the harbormaster your letter. He's never seen one like it nor heard of someone coming back. I asked how to get a letter to you, and he gave me no hope, but what else can I do? I am addressing this to you on the merchant ship Atalanta. The harbormaster will give it to the next westbound ship.*

He told me that Atalanta sails from Baltimore, but she was here from France. Her captain reported losing men and spare rigging when she was boarded by a British warship and that he must have been desperate for crew. He can't be arrested unless he returns to Marblehead and you're on board as evidence of his crime. So, please be wary! Your captain will either throw you off in some foreign port or overboard. Or he'll not come back here.

Eamon, how do I do this? How do I live between hoping and not knowing? It took four months for your letter to reach me, and you were gone two months before sending it. Am I writing to a corpse? You are correct, I cannot picture where you are, cannot imagine what it is like. Maybe I should be glad for that. The more I learn, the more hopeless it sounds.

We are indebted to our neighbors that I haven't already lost the business. When you vanished, they let me help with their harvests else I'd not accept their charity, not share what they gave up from their own tables. This spring, they've helped me plant a small garden of my own. It was a harsh winter, but Alex and Amy started a log-splitting venture after school. Maggie's oldest, Ben, showed Alex how to use our axe. Every day, he knocked on doors and split logs for people. They gave him a few pieces of firewood for his help, and Amy went with him. He had a regular route. It made him strong, kept us warm, and gave them both a sense of pride. He's a regular little man now, his adolescence stolen. Amy, though, still treats this as an adventure from a storybook. Blessedly, she's still a child, if only for a little longer.

One evening a week, I teach the adults who want to learn to read and write. I started this between the quilting bees and knitting groups. Maggie's youngest son, Timothy, helps me and Alex in the shop. He is a voracious reader. He would work free for the loan of our books, but I pay him for his hours. And I've *started a weekly news that's going well. Zachary Silvers makes deliveries for us. He fixes things on the house or in the shop when I can't. He's good help. Mister Anderson orders more printing than the bank needs, and I'm painfully aware that he's a widower. The baker gives us a pastry most days as well.*

I don't know what else to tell you. I ask myself how long I can wait for you, how long I can last. And, to be honest, I don't know the answer. I look to scripture for help and feel abandoned. And bitter. I don't even know if you're still alive. You got into a fight? And they say Cape Horn has claimed hundreds of ships. Eamon, do you realize how much I miss you? What I'm saying is hurry. Please hurry. If you're still out there, please come back to us soon. And if you're not . . . I swear I will survive. At least until the children are safely on their way, into lives of their own (if anything is safe anymore).

Your loving wife,

Becca

When did I start crying? Eamon asks himself. He slumps to sit on the knighthead and shakes his head. There are two more notes in the envelope.

Dear Papa,

Where are you? Mama reads your letter to me most days. So, I know you are on a ship in faraway places, that you didn't want to go, and that you will come back. And I know you miss me. I miss you too. When will you come home? Will you bring something back for me? I'm singing at church now, and I play with Missus Holbrook's chickens and goats. One just had a baby (goat, not chicken). Alex and I chopped wood for people. We've made many new friends. Everyone knows us, and they want our help so they can help us. Do you know what I mean? I read faster than ever now. There are so many stories to read, but the stories I want are the ones you will tell when you tuck me in. Come home as soon as you can.

I love you,
Amy

16 April 1811
Dear Father,

We worry about you. Mother most of all. I'm sure you worry about us, too, but as far as I can see, worrying doesn't help. And neither does prayer. Sometimes we are too busy to worry anyway.

You would be glad to see how much help we get from everyone in town. We give as much back as we can. Last winter, I split wood for people. After Ben showed me how to do it, I got good with the axe. Amy and I brought a little firewood home in return. She learned to balance each log on a stump, get out of the way, and pick up what I split. She piled what we took home on her sled, and when I didn't let her ride on the sled, she pulled it with me. With spring here and summer coming, there's other work. I'll find whatever it is. And who knows, maybe you'll be back soon.

I help in the shop when I can. I could help more, but mother won't let me stop going to school, even though I'm the best student there. I even help the teacher with the younger kids. It's geography I like most, now that you're out there somewhere.

I hope you come home soon. We all miss you and will be much happier when you are here, where you belong, with us. Give my respects to Coop and Mister Holbrook, please.

Your son,
Alex

"He sounds so grown up!" Eamon wants to reread each letter, but tears blur his vision. He also wants to keep them hidden. For the first time since waking on board, he holds precious things. He knows that they make him vulnerable. What if these are taken away, if he loses them or they get soaked? He steels himself for this loss and intends to burn every letter into his memory so that this testament to his real self cannot be taken from him. Until then, until he knows every word, can conjure the color of the paper, recall the feel of it, and trace the edges of each page with his inner eye, he will be careful.

Eamon feels lonelier yet buoyed at the same time. The air through which he sees the lights on shore feels new. They shine their reflections on the water like upside-down candles.

When the other shore boat bumps alongside in the dark, Eamon catches their lines. Half the crew stumbles aboard. Some have swollen lips and black eyes. All are drunk. The rest are still ashore—in the arms of a whore, on the floor of a jail, or sleeping the rum off in some corner of an alley.

"Are you good?" Sam asks through his own haze as he climbs aboard.

"Aye, very well. Why d'you ask?"

"I don' know." He shrugs. "Dunno."

"Have you got a minute?"

"Hell," Sam answers louder than Eamon wants, "I've got hours and days, months, and years."

Sam follows Eamon to the bow. Eamon warns him to stay quiet. He pulls Maggie's letter from his pocket. "It's from Maggie."

Sam covers his mouth. Suddenly sober, wide-eyed, he looks back and forth between Eamon and the letter. Shaken, he whispers, "How'd that get here?" Eamon tells him of the bosun's help.

15 April, Year of our Lord, 1811
Sam, my dear old mule,

It was grand to get your letter. We were worried about you and still are. We're relieved to learn you're still alive, or at least you were when Eamon wrote it for you. Whenever a ship comes into the harbor, one of us goes to see who it is and if there's another letter or if it's yourself coming home.

The harvest was enough to share with Rebecca. The winter was bitter cold, but we had plenty of wood, and young Alex split it for us. After your letters arrived, we all got together for a dinner to celebrate. Some townsfolk heard about it, joined in, and before you knew it, the house was full, and we started singing. We drank to your health (maybe a little too much). You would have loved it.

I sold a cow and have logged some woods. Haven't had to sell any land yet. Ben's been doing us proud and has done the planting this spring. He's starting to call on Eleanor Smith too. Jacob has been out and about too much. He doesn't listen to Ben like he would to you, but he's here when we need him, and Timothy, too, when he's not helping Rebecca. Elizabeth is the teacher's favorite, and she helps with more chores. She's kind with Amy and includes her in chores and play.

Rebecca is teaching some of us to read and write. She says I could write this note myself. Maybe I will next time, if there is a next time. Maybe it doesn't matter. Putting a note in a bottle is what it feels like. At least it gives us something to do, something to hope for.

Imagine, you, a doctor! What I cannot picture is where you are and what it's like. And so much ocean! Instead, I imagine you walking through this door.

We all love you and pray for your safe return soon. Be careful.

Yours truly,

Maggie

Eamon is cautious with Coop's letter. The boy might not be discrete. But he's not a "boy" anymore. Still, the crew envies Coop's

youth. They swear he doesn't pay for a drink or a prostitute. The
barmaids light up when they see a young "innocent" come in the
door. Relative to the rest of the scarred and weathered men, he is
gorgeous. So, it's no surprise to Eamon that Coop doesn't return to
the ship until morning, just in time for the day's work.

As usual, Coop presents his newest tattoo: a full-rigged ship on
his chest. "To show I've been 'round the Horn."

"At this pace, you might run out of room, Coop. You haven't put
any on your back yet."

"I don't know if my scars can be tattooed, and another beating
would ruin 'em. Besides, I couldn't see 'em there."

"There *is* that. Do you want to show them off when you get
home?"

Coop pauses. "Eamon, I'm never goin' back. Or if I am, I'll be a
sailor by then. Maybe even a captain, if I learn to navigate."

Eamon smiles back and shakes his head. "And you'd be a good
captain, Coop. But your home will be poorer for your absence. Your
family will miss you. Do you miss them?"

"Of course. But I'm not the same as I was. Who knows? Maybe
I could homeport from there. That way, I would see them between
sailings."

When the day's chores are assigned, Coop's are up in the rigging.
It's the one place where Eamon might talk with him privately; he
speaks up to work aloft also.

"Coop, listen, I've got something to tell you, and I need you to
keep it secret." Coop looks up, curious. "Keep working, now. No one's
to know about this. Except you and Sam." Coop nods, and they keep
at their chores. "I've been sending letters home from every port. I
don't know if they make it, but I keep writing them anyway. I've been
writing letters for Sam, too, and he takes them to the harbormaster
or the other ships. So, the first one got through, and yesterday, I got
a letter back from Rebecca. From Alex and Amy too." Coop stops his
work and stares at Eamon. "Keep working." He waits a moment. "Sam

got one from Maggie too. Those letters mean the world to me, Coop. I can't tell you how much. I think I've already memorized them. Even if I lost them, I'd still have them. Almost."

Coop looks up again. "Good for you! How are they?"

"They're faring well enough. Maggie has been generous helping Becca. She still has the print shop, and Alex sends his regards. He and Amy have been picking up chores around town."

"Eamon, I'm happy for you. Don't worry, I won't tell anyone."

"Of course, you wouldn't. Or you wouldn't mean to. But would you not tell anyone if there's a letter for you too?" This brings Coop up short.

> *17 April, Year of our Lord, 1811*
> *Dear son,*
>
> *Your mother and I heard from Rebecca McGrath where you are. We pray you're taking care of yourself. You're a hard worker, we miss your help, and we are sure anyone you work for will appreciate you too. But please be careful and come back to us. Until then, could you write to us? Just a short note. Anything to let us know you're still alive. Please.*
>
> *This has been hardest on your mother. She's never been strong, but she's been sickly ever since you disappeared. Maybe it would be easier if you weren't our only child. These have been hard, sad days without you.*
>
> *I'm busy trying to keep up without an apprentice, so I've not been much help to her. To give her more care, I would need to let go of some work, to slow down. Instead, I'm always building the business up to support us and your family too, when you start one.*
>
> *The brewery in Salem might want me to partner with them. In which case, I'll need an apprentice anyway. The blacksmith has recommended a few young men, but I don't want to teach them our trade only to let them go when you*

get back. And them to compete with us.

Where are you? What is it like there? I cannot fathom.

I pray you are still alive and will come back to us soon.

That would be a happy day. We could use some happy days.

I hope this letter finds its way to you.

Don't forget us and take care of yourself,

Your father.

CHAPTER 15

HONG KONG IS the largest, most densely populated city *Atalanta* has called upon. Fires for cooking and industry choke the air with smoke. The harbor is plied by flocks of small boats. The wood they are made of is golden in color. Their bows and sterns are squared off and rise well above their waists, where a round-roofed cabin sits. Their sails have several battens for their entire width and are almost square. A quarter of each sail protrudes forward of its canted mast. Those boats without sails wiggle across the water while a man at the stern stands and sculls a sweep.

Eamon follows Captain Rolinson up a street crowded by people hurrying in every direction. Close behind, the two biggest men from the crew follow as bodyguards; Mister Duncan looks the part while Sam tries to. The four of them follow a man sent by the new owners of *Atalanta*. Their guide wears a dark-blue jacket over a loose, long-sleeved gown. The gown is tied at the waist and has a slit on each side from ankle to thigh, revealing dark leggings beneath. His shoes look like slippers that upturn to a slight point. He has a thin mustache and beard. Eamon is distracted by the tip of the man's long, thin braid swinging back and forth above his hips. Almost all the local men have this queue while the fronts of their heads are shaved bald. Most wear close-fitting cloth caps of dark blue.

The nearness of the bustling sea of people, the open grills and wafting aromas, the cacophony, and the apparent hurry challenge Eamon. What distracts him most is the sound of children. He hears their laughter and glimpses bright, shy eyes full of curiosity. The streets are narrow. Some are cobbled, others covered in thick grass mats. The rest are hard, packed dirt. The walls, doors, and windows hemming them in are forested with signs, their bright colors tarnished. Most are made of cloth. As a printer, Eamon studies them when he can steal a glance. They are all posted vertically, and the local script on them is dynamic, sweeping. *Handsome*, he thinks.

The heavy leather portfolio full of *Atalanta's* logs and manifests taxes him. The captain had impressed upon his three men the need to carry themselves with purpose. They are not to gawk no matter how novel anything may be. But as soon as Eamon started walking, he became dizzy and knew he was in trouble. He is used to unending motion, outrageous sometimes and subtle others. His muscles are attuned to the isometrics of balance, even in his sleep, but *not* on an unmoving surface. He would be steadier if the ground were quaking beneath him. Also, shoes feel unnatural to him by now, and having walked no more than *Atalanta's* length for months, he is out of breath. So, he stumbles, and Sam steadies him.

They arrive at a closed bamboo gate in a tall stone wall. On either side of it, a guard stands, each armed with a spear in one hand and resting his other hand on the hilt of a long sword at his belt. Their guide barks something to the guards whereupon they open the gate. The captain and crew enter a clean, spacious courtyard and pause before four wide steps leading up to the veranda of a large house. When the gate behind them closes, the hush within these walls contrasts with the commotion of the streets.

Their guide bows to them. "Weh-come to Asia Oceanic. Sank you fo' joining us. Now we ah' inside, you mus' give me you weapons, p'ease." He holds out his hands, and the captain nods. As Mister Duncan and Sam disarm, a young man enters the courtyard from nearby. The guide passes the weapons to this assistant, who then leaves the courtyard. He claps his hands twice. On cue, four women approach. They wear long, colorfully decorated, narrow silk gowns and pale face paint. Averting their eyes, taking small rapid steps, each carries a wooden bucket and a white cloth. The guide points to the steps behind the men. "P'ease sit and 'emove shoes. Woo-men to assist you." When captain and crew sit on the steps, each woman kneels before one of them, reaches for his feet, and unlaces his boots. The woman attending the chief mate removes a knife tucked into the top of his right boot. They set aside the men's ragged shoes.

Sam startles when the woman before him begins washing his feet. Eamon, still dizzy, is transfixed by his attendant, by her fragrance, her touch, her entire devotion to her movement. She is unhurried yet efficient. She looks fragile yet strong with purpose. Her nearness feels like a drug that leaves him confused and, curiously, afraid. To finish, the attendants slip white cloth slippers onto the men's feet, stand, and step back, eyes on the ground and heads bowed.

Feeling awkward, the men stand. Sam begins, "Well, I'll be . . ." The captain cuts him off with a glance. Still, Sam imitates the women's slight bow. Eamon does the same, not sure if he catches a peek of eye contact from the woman who attends him.

Their guide takes to the steps, the captain turns to follow, and his men join him. Before them are latticed walls of paper and bamboo panels. These are revealed to be doors when their guide slides open the middle two. "Gent'men, 'iss way." From this room, they follow into another larger room where a long low table is surrounded by pillows on the floor. They are motioned to sit around one end of the table. "We begin wis food and jink," their guide announces and claps his hands again. Another wall slides open. Servants bring in trays of tea service, bowls of soup, and small enameled dishes with steaming rice, vegetables, and fish. There are small ceramic spoons adjacent to bowls of soup. The only other utensils the men see are chopsticks, whereupon their bellies growl and they consider eating with bare hands. As if their minds have been read, the women who attended them at their entrance come in. They are to pour tea and otherwise attend each man.

"Captain, sir, is this how shipping companies do business?" Sam asks.

"There are formalities to follow here. However meaningless this may be, it would be rude to go against its grain."

"Lord forbid we should be rude, sir." Sam smiles.

"Is it meaningless, sir?" Mister Duncan asks. "Looks like a good sign to me."

"It would be disrespectful to hurry through this. But until we get our pay, our next sailing, and back aboard the ship, nothing is certain. For now, there is no way around this."

"Thank heavens for that." Sam can't help himself.

"Sam," Eamon points out, "all of a sudden, you sound religious."

"I might be, with an angel like this."

The old man is impatient to meet *Atalanta*'s new owners, but to his men, the afternoon passes quickly. Their misuse of chopsticks proves laughable and their attendants' help essential. From one sleeve, each woman produces a fan and fans the man she attends. By the time two panels slide open and three men enter, the captain and crew are sated. Only the fermented wine is not cleared from the table, and they are feeling its effects. The men coming in are European, but their attire is Asian: lightweight breeches under a thin, loose-fitting gown that reaches to their ankles and cloth slippers, all of it black. The captain and crew are stiff as they stand. In contrast, the courtesans seem to rise without effort and float across the room to leave.

"Captain Rolinson," one man addresses him and reaches to shake his hand. "It's a pleasure to meet you, sir, and see our ship in harbor. Your passage went well, I take it."

"Yes, sir. She's a fine ship. We would have been here sooner, but the orders I received left me sway."

"Indeed, I trust you made use of that sway. This is Mister Cohen, our accountant, Mister Levi, my partner, and I am Mister Ames. Our agent was most encouraging about *Atalanta*. We will bring a shipwright with us tomorrow to assess her ourselves."

"Of course, sir. I'm sure you will be pleased with her."

"You've been her master since she launched, I believe."

"That's right, sir. Ten years now, with most of our trade in the Atlantic and Eastern Pacific. She may carry a little less cargo than some ships, but she's faster than most."

"Yes, her lines are new to us, and we're counting on her speed." Mister Ames pauses and looks from the captain to his crew.

"This is my first mate, sir, Mister Duncan. Able seaman Sam, and Eamon McGrath is the ship's purser."

Ames tips his head. "Please, let's sit. I trust your afternoon has been pleasant."

"Indeed, sir. Thank you very much."

"If it hasn't passed too much so, shall we get to work, or may we start in the morning?"

"Not at all, sir. We can start now."

"Very well. Mister Duncan and Sam need not attend unless you wish."

"No, sir, that's right. They'll not mind waiting before your man escorts us back to the ship."

"Nonsense. You could *all* use a rest. Please plan on staying the night. We have guest rooms. After this meeting, Misters Cohen, Levi, and I will confer. We will have orders for you soon. Our longshoremen are ready to offload tomorrow. The shipyard is standing by for any work. I'm sure you have a list. We'll reload *Atalanta* in the days after they're done. We can turn you around in short order save for a suitable leave for your men."

"That won't be necessary, sir. We can be ready to sail in a few days."

"You're short on crew, Captain, and had a long passage. Perhaps you should heed our preparations. To keep your crew and add to it."

The captain's voice steels, saying, "I can explain that in these logs."

"Yes, I'm sure you can. For now, though, we will send word to your second mate to expect you tomorrow. No doubt he stands by on board."

Captain Rolinson pauses before answering, "Aye, sir. Shall we begin?"

CHAPTER 16

EAMON USHERS HIS courtesan out of the room she shows him to and slides the door closed behind her. He turns to survey his accommodations and revels in being alone for the first time in over a year. A spacious mattress is in the middle of the floor. He cannot remember sleeping on a motionless bed. When he sits upon it, it feels firm. Rubbing the edge of the sheets between thumb and forefinger is his first time touching silk. A low table is at the head of the bed. On it is a quill, bowl of ink, sheaf of paper, and a dish holding a burning candle. *After all, I am the "purser."* He can sit on the edge of the bed and still write at the table. *Becca will note the paper.* By the table is a bucket of water, a ladle, and a ceramic cup. He turns the cup in his hand to admire its dark-blue glaze and pattern. Exploring further, he notes two buckets in a corner of the room, one with water and a white cloth draped across it, the other with a lid. *My chamber pot.* Thin grass mats are at the entrance to the room and beside the bed and buckets.

The room strikes him as spare yet luxurious. He compares the smooth bamboo floor to the hard, packed dirt of his childhood home. *How long have they lived like this? At least my children have a wood floor. If only they could see this. How can I describe it to them?*

It had been a long meeting. He is impressed at the details Mister Ames selected from the logs and manifests. His questions were precise, especially when it came to the British Navy stealing crew and spare rigging. Eamon wonders if Ames was, himself, a captain. Where had he learned his trade? Or who was the captain who tutored him? Reviewing the logbook, when he came to the new mizzen topmast, he asked after its rigging and sails. Then there was the trading to account for and the stores on board. Eamon knows all the words and numbers came from his pen. He even remembers most of them but has nothing to compare them to. As the meeting went on, it became obvious that the new owners of *Atalanta* have many comparisons to measure them against.

His head is swimming as he sits. Surrounded by comfort, he feels he could sleep for a month. Before writing to Becca, he tests the mattress for a minute, gets his breeches off, and lies back, still wearing his drawers and shirt. He swims partially to consciousness when deft hands finish sliding him under the silk and prop a small pillow under his head.

In bright morning light, he doesn't remember falling asleep. He had thought to sleep in his drawers but must've been too tired to remember undressing. He is surprised to have a headache. The wine had seemed harmless. Feeling in a fog, his eyelids close until he thinks, *where* are *my clothes?* He sits up, rubs his eyes, and looks around. "What the devil? They're gone!"

Following a gentle knock, a door slides open. His courtesan enters. *Has she been spying on me?* She slides the door closed behind her, turns, and approaches in that smooth grace of hers. She carries a robe to his bedside and waits.

He clutches the top sheet to his torso. "What now? Do you know where my clothes are?"

She averts her eyes and holds the robe out for him to slip into. Something more catches his attention, something in her expression.

"What is it? Is something wrong?"

Kneeling, she drops, level with him. She releases a shoulder of the robe from one hand to reach behind him. Her eyes meet his. This time, she does not lower her gaze. Her expression is pained. He almost jumps clear of her when her fingers trace the network of scars on his back. She winces and shakes her head.

"It's not that bad. It was, but not anymore. The cat-o'nine-tails.

A whipping." He tips his head to one side. "Why am I telling you? Do you speak English?" Her eyes are questioning now. "But it doesn't feel like you don't understand." He cannot pull away from her touch on his back. It has been too long since anyone has touched him with tenderness. He wants to lean into it. "Maybe you're pretending and you're fluent." He closes his eyes and waits, but she says nothing. He holds up his hand. "Wait. Please." She hesitates and withdraws, stands back up, and again proffers the robe. Feeling awkward, he manages to stand and get into the robe modestly before letting the sheet drop.

"There. What next?" When he turns, she is already walking toward the door, glancing back and beckoning. Barefoot, he follows her to a covered breezeway that borders a gravel courtyard. The gravel has been raked into a pattern. A large, striated boulder stands off-center in the yard by a small maple tree. The tree has lost most of its leaves, yet there isn't a leaf upon the gravel. Eamon follows his attendant down the breezeway's slight incline. She slides a lacquered paper door open and stands aside. Before him is a deep tub of water, steam rising from its surface. Two small stools stand beside it, one with towels atop, a small pitcher next to the other. Beyond it, a mattress on the floor. On another stool near where he stands, his clothes are washed and folded next to his boots, clean beyond recognition.

"Bless you! Sam's right. This may be heaven."

She steps into the room behind him, slides the door closed, and stands with eyes downcast.

"Oh no. This is . . . I can't . . . I mean, I'm a married man." Running a hand through his hair, he adds, "I would kill for this bath, but you must wait outside." She still stands there. "Please." He reaches around her to slide the door open and motions for her to step outside. She complies. "Thank heavens. Now I can enjoy this. I'm sure you'll be waiting. Out here. Thank you." He slides the door shut and then reopens it to ask, "What is your name?" Pointing back and forth, he says, "Name. Eamon. My name is Eamon. Your name is . . . name: Eamon. Name?"

"Mingzhu," comes the whisper. Pointing to herself, she says, "Mingzhu." Pointing to him, she says, "Ay-men."

"Ming-zoo," he repeats and bows his head. "Thank you, Ming-zoo. Now, if you'll excuse me." He slides the door shut again. "Saints be praised, I might get religious too."

Later, back aboard *Atalanta*, he wonders how she knew of the scars on his back.

CHAPTER 17

WITH THE MATES supervising, off-loading proceeds apace aboard *Atalanta*. They post a man at the forecastle and one at the galley saying the "Chinamen" are not to be trusted. It is a swarm of locals from dawn to dusk. The bosun stands by the gangway to record every item offloaded. Eamon does the same on the waterside, where small boats arrive empty and depart fully laden. Both of them are followed by a severe employee of the company. These bark orders to the coolies in Mandarin and use a curious frame with rows of beads.

At the end of the day, the longshoremen vanish into the throngs of the city. Most of the crew follows suit, beckoned by a host of locals toward the satisfaction of their thirsts. A Chinese guard lolls about at the shore end of *Atalanta*'s gangplank. With the ship tied to a dock, the captain sees fit to have a watch fore and aft. Eamon and Spanky trade places from one end of the ship to the other. As they pass, they chat. The only other people aboard are the captain with his courtesan and Cook.

"So, you got the short straw, Spanky?"

"Don't worry. Swede will relieve me soon."

"Do you think he'll be sober enough to find his way back?"

"He's more interested in women than he is in drink. But you, it had to make you crazy." Spanky catches himself. "I mean, always confined to the ship."

"I've turned into a monk by now."

"Surely, you're defrocked after last night. It's unnatural to go too long without a woman. Unhealthy."

"What's unhealthy is the way the mate treated his woman." Eamon had been shocked. "Even with a split lip and black eye, she managed to look pretty and be kind."

"Aye, he was braggin' about her. Made my mouth water, it did. Mind you, not the part about slappin' her around."

"She sat beside him at the table and served him as if nothing had happened, even laced his boots when we left."

"That's talent, that is. What was yours like?"

Eamon thinks better of arguing against the mate's entitlement. *Let them think I'm daft, but don't let them think I'm weak.* To escape the conversation, he agrees. "More talent than you can imagine. It was a night I'll not forget." *Having slept through it.* He heads for the other end of the deck.

"Aw, c'mon Eamon," Spanky pleads to his back. "What was she like?"

Eamon holds up a flat hand without looking back and shakes his head.

In two days, *Atalanta's* holds are empty, and she is moved to a shipway. There is scraping, caulking, and painting to do, rigging and sails to replace. With the ship no longer afloat, everything on board is motionless and feels "wrong." Eamon's vertigo returns. The men swell full of themselves, working alongside a swarm of laborers who know their work better than the sailors do. Still, it isn't uncommon to hear someone saying, "No, not like that. 'Ere, give me that. Now, watch." Their words may not be understood, but their gestures are. Vasco points at things and swears he has a bilingual finger.

There is another ship alongside the yard. The sight of her stops *Atalanta's* crew. Even Eamon, ignorant of what he sees, falls silent. Jack answers his unasked question. "Typhoon," he says. "From the looks of her, she's lucky she made it." All that remains of the bowsprit are splinters. The foremast is gone too. Jagged wood shows where chainplates were ripped out of her now shattered bulwarks. Where sails should be furled, tatters of cloth stream from a yardarm . . . if there is a yardarm at all. All her upper masts are gone. The spanker's gaff too. There are no longboats on deck; their davits are bent beyond use. Bare wood is exposed where paint was scoured off by wind and water. With no one on board, the exhausted ship looks haunted.

"We are tiny," Eamon mutters.

When the crew takes their leave at the end of each day, they gamble their pay away or spend it on whores and drink or souvenirs and the clothes they need. Mornings, the company's guide and a few guards go to the jails to look for those who haven't returned. Rye is found slain in an alley, apparently sliced with one of those long swords. Despite losses, *Atalanta*'s roster grows. Where before the captain stole men from their lives, the company now sends sailors for him to pick from. Eamon sees some dregs among the men who request permission to come aboard. Sailors who have been left behind by other ships hail from all over the world.

After five days, the ship is afloat again and back at the company wharf. It is midday, hot, and muggy. Amid the continuing work above and below decks, the captain summons Eamon.

"Sir?"

The captain holds out the ship's empty leather attaché. "The company's man will be here to escort you. Take this with you."

"Yes, sir."

"I expect they'll send you back with our manifest. I'm staying aboard. We begin loading tomorrow and will be at anchor in a few days." He pauses. "Answer only what they ask. Do not volunteer unnecessary information."

CHAPTER 18

I SUPPOSE HE is not so ugly, Mingzhu thinks. *Maybe I am getting used to him. At least he is better than Tu's monster, but what am I doing wrong that he does not want me?*

At the long table, Eamon sits and drinks tea with Mingzhu seated close by. She teaches chopstick technique while he attempts to eat from a small dish of rice and fish. Intensely aware of her proximity, he is glad for an innocent pursuit between them. Still, he notices her robe is more revealing today. As he fumbles another morsel, she stifles another laugh.

When the sight of her arrests him at last, he shakes his head. "My Lord, look at you."

She drops her gaze.

No knock precedes a shoji screen sliding open and Mister Ames's entrance. Startled, Eamon begins to get up as the man lowers himself to take a place on the opposite side of the table. "No, that's quite all right. Please, sit. How are you today?"

"Very well, sir, thank you. And you?"

Mingzhu stands, bows, and backs out of the room.

"Thank you for asking. I am well. And pleased with our purchase of *Atalanta*."

"Am I to take our manifest back, sir?"

"Indeed. We will begin loading tea, porcelains, and silks tomorrow. You should be back underway in three days." Mister Ames pauses.

"Very well, sir. Is there anything else?"

"Perhaps you could tell me, Mister McGrath. *Is* there anything else?"

Eamon, unaccustomed to being formally addressed, feels the hairs on the back of his neck rise. "Sir, my impression is that you do not ask questions for which you do not have answers."

"But is there a question *you* would ask?"

"As a matter of fact, sir, there is. What matters to me is whether we are east or westbound and if we shall reach the American states again. If not, I would ask if there is another ship bound there and if I might sign on to her."

"No doubt *Atalanta* will call on America again, but whether you sail east or west is all the same from the opposite side of the earth. I do not expect another of our ships to arrive soon, and I assume that you are not willing to wait for one." Again, he pauses. "Mister McGrath, the logs of *Atalanta* change markedly after her visit to Marblehead. They note four new crewmen signing on, you among them."

"No, sir." Eamon can't stop his bitter tone. "I did *not* sign on."

"There." Mister Ames tries to finish Eamon's sentence. "You did not sign on *there*?"

"No, sir. Nor anywhere else. I was shanghaied from Marblehead, taken from my family and my trade. Along with Sam, Coop, and Jack. There was another taken with us, but he never woke up." As he speaks, he recalls the captain's warning to not volunteer information.

"I see. *Atalanta was* shorthanded after she was boarded by the British Navy." Mister Ames sighs, leans back, and tilts his head to study Eamon. "What was your trade?"

"I was a printer, sir. And intend to be again."

"So, you intend to return to your former life."

"Or die trying."

"How dramatic. No doubt, Captain Rolinson is aware of this."

"Very aware. Following my first attempt to jump ship, he has denied me shore leave."

"That's a shame. The records you keep make my job easier. And perhaps more interesting, it appears."

"It's your ship, sir. I suppose you've paid for the entertainment."

"Yes, I have, haven't I?"

"Yes, as you've also paid for our concubines." Eamon nods toward Mingzhu's exit.

"Indeed. Quite as I pay your wage. Is something amiss with that?"

"Why would I find anything amiss with being taken from my family? With their going into servitude? With my dying before I can get back to them? Why would I find anything wrong with your part in the prostitution of this woman and the mate's abuse of his?"

"It's a different world than you knew, isn't it? You would have me change it, but I did not start the practice of kidnapping men nor was I the author of China's caste system. These pieces were long in place before my time. They are the waters I navigate my company through."

"True, sir, but they are waters with which you are complicit. Your profits are based on this system. Why would you change anything?"

"Your experience is a crime, Mister McGrath. I'll grant you that, but I am not the criminal who committed it. You imagine where you would be if you were not here. I doubt you can imagine where Mingzhu would be if she were not. You were lucky once, but now you know what unlucky is. Would you believe her life has gone the opposite way of yours? From unlucky to lucky. From a brothel to a shipping company. Her coworker may not fare as well at the hands of Mister Duncan, but when he leaves, she herself will be cared for."

"If she's still alive by then?"

"Ah, yes. Hopefully it won't come to that. I have an investment in her, like I do in *Atalanta*, and in you, and I am in the habit of protecting my investments. Even the one I have in the first mate. I expect some losses, but as long as the profits outrun them, I am in business."

"I see." Eamon hears the edge in his own voice but can't stop now. "I see that the shipping business enslaves its crews and that 'courtesan' is a kind word for whore, but there are no kind words for murder and whipping and rape."

"Mingzhu tells us your back bears the scars of a terrible beating."

"A beating for which you paid, sir."

Mister Ames hesitates but does not flinch. "Your civilization, too, has its underbelly. I wonder in which parts *you* are complicit. At least my ships don't carry slaves. Nor opium. Perhaps what I *can* change is your mind about getting off my payroll. When it comes to profits and losses, I'd rather not lose a ship's purser."

"Pardon me, sir, but there isn't enough money to change my mind."

"As you can see, I have more than money to offer, and I'm not trying to keep you from your family. What if I give you safe passage to and from Marblehead in exchange for your employ? There's no reason you cannot have a home there and a home here too. You could support your family and advance in our fleet."

"Sir, there isn't anything I'll not do to return to my family, even if that means working for you. But if I reach them, I will not sail again."

Ames raises one eyebrow. "As you said, though, I pay for the entertainment. I can give you safe passage, or I can put you at great risk. I could fire you here and now and have you followed to see how far you get. Or I could ship you out in the first mate's watch and await news." Eamon wonders to himself how Mister Ames learned of *that*. "If you get back to your family, I wonder what you will find. Even if home waits for you, has it not changed? Have you not changed?" Mister Ames lets his questions hang a moment and stands to leave. "You have a few days to consider my offer." Eamon doesn't rise. "In the meantime, please avail yourself of our comforts. If Mingzhu is not to your taste, perhaps you'd rather have a boy attend you." His casual tone leaves Eamon confused and then speechless. He goes on without missing a beat, "No? Very well, we will fill your attaché and send you back to your ship before nightfall. Good day." As he leaves, Mingzhu enters.

Within the next few hours, Eamon faces that, indeed, Mister Ames has more than money to offer. While he again soaks in a hot bath, Mingzhu reenters the room, averts her eyes, and holds out a robe to him again. Through gestures, she leads him to lie prone and covered on a futon. As she massages him, he falls asleep. He awakes enough to turn over as she directs. Half dreaming, he is embarrassed and hisses a curse when the sheet covering him reveals his erection. She lays a hand on his chest to quiet him and reaches her other hand under the cover. His eyes meet and search hers. She continues to hold him. He feels paralyzed. She withdraws and disrobes. He lowers his gaze to drink in her smooth skin, small breasts, nipples, and flat stomach. She slips under the cover to lay the length of herself against him. He wraps an arm around her and begins to tremble. Taken aback, he whispers, "What's happening? Why am I shaking?"

Pulling back enough to see fear and confusion in his eyes, Mingzhu shushes his question. He quakes for many minutes. "I don't know what this is. Have you done something to me?" She meets this with soft words, the meaning of which he can only intuit. Whatever they are, he feels permission to let go, to give up. His tears come and go and come again. He breathes in gasps. His release of trauma slowly passes. Only then does she straddle him, leaning close over him, making sure he can caress and kiss her wherever he wants. He sits up with her in his lap, her legs wrapped around him. He presses her harder to himself, as if she cannot be close enough.

"How did I forget this?" Afterwards, he falls asleep with Mingzhu naked at his side.

❊ ❊ ❊

Stepping out of the gate into the dusk light, the attaché full and slung across his torso, Eamon feels boneless, dizzy, lost. He recalls when his sea legs were unused to shore, but this spinning is internal. Life was simpler this morning. As it was before the view from atop

Atalanta's masts. He feels what? Conflict and relief, together. Gratitude? To Mingzhu. And beyond her, to what? It is all he can do to focus on the guide's quick pace through the fading light. Arriving at the ship feels like a surprise. He doesn't remember any of the path he just walked.

Over the three days it takes to load *Atalanta*'s new cargo and move her back to a mooring, Eamon's recall of his recent pleasures won't leave him alone. *Hell, what if I don't make it home? I may never see Becca again. And if I go back to Mingzhu, no one other than she and I will know. There is Ames . . . and God, but what God? Why should I forswear myself? I am a man, after all.* At the end of each day, when the crew heads into the city, when the company's escort arrives dockside to deliver the captain's courtesan, Eamon feels hungry for Mingzhu's touch. Until the ship departs, he casts guilt aside, the captain gives him leave, and he follows the escort back to the company.

CHAPTER 19

AFTER TWELVE DAYS in port, the contrast between life on land and life at sea is stark. *What an illusion.* Eamon shakes his head. *On solid ground, we pretend to control, but the sea lays bare that control is an illusion. Our choices are fewer out here, but they are more important to us. We adapt only to adapt again. We respond, we influence, but we never control.*

Recalling the sounds of children, the feel of a motionless bed, a hot bath, and Minghzu's touch, Eamon looks back and asks the shore itself, "When will I see you again?" He imagines the shore asks the same of him, but the shore he imagines is not this one, and for the first time, he is sailing toward it instead of away. This makes a colossal difference. For most of the crew, everywhere is anywhere. With no home to sail to or from, all of it is nowhere.

A ship full of men working as if their lives depend upon it (because their lives do, indeed, depend upon it) has a clarity Eamon did not appreciate before. *Atalanta* has a full crew of over forty now. More disparate than ever, it includes three Asians. The captain and mates are suspicious of these, irritated by their poor English and lack of experience, but Mister Ames insisted they sign on. At least their Chinese names are easily butchered to Tommy, Yow, and Hero, and they work hard to prove themselves. A new man makes up for whatever these three lack. One of three Africans aboard, he keeps to himself. Tall, imposing, and very black, his name is Moses. Weathered and scarred, he wears sea time like a cloak, as if he belongs at sea and knows it. He is capable at every task and shies from none.

Chips, Cook, and Swede now attend to their particular duties rather than pulling lines, going aloft, or steering. Eamon spends most of his daylight hours noting and correcting details on new charts. These give Captain Rolinson a priceless advantage over competing captains. Entrusted to him by Mr. Ames, these charts are more valuable than all of *Atalanta*'s cargo. They are kept under lock and key. Even so, their accuracy shall be constantly confirmed and updated. Newly interested in *Atalanta*'s progress, Eamon watches her track across the charts, surprised by how many details escaped him when he was consumed with bitterness.

Atalanta's approach to Hong Kong had been through the Solomon Islands. She left New Guinea and the Spanish-held Phillipines to port. Crossing the tropics in the North Pacific, she escaped typhoon season unscathed. Now southbound on the South China Sea, a mix of winds and calms renews a concern: pirates. Mister Ames had assured the captain that the most successful pirate fleet had retired two years ago.

"Retired?" Rolinson was compelled to ask.

"Yes. The pirate queen amassed a navy that gave her the leverage to negotiate amnesty."

"The most powerful pirate was a woman?"

"It was. She commanded over fifty thousand pirates and more than a thousand ships," Ames explained. "Still, in case anyone is noting your departure, I'll have a warship escort you for your first days underway."

Captain Rolinson guesses that some of those same pardoned pirates are in the crew of their escort. When they wave goodbye, he doesn't regret seeing them go and orders the longboats launched and towed. There is nowhere to hide at sea. If becalmed, a full crew can row *Atalanta* away from an enemy. At least an approaching pirate would have to row as well. Rich or poor, large or small, threatened or threatening, nature is indifferent to them all.

On an open ocean, months can pass without seeing land or

another ship. By comparison, the South China Sea seems crowded. Once, under full sail with no wind, the captain orders the anchor lowered to keep from drifting toward a reef. Another time, *Atalanta* anchors behind an archipelago for the night rather than maneuver through it in the dark. In daylight, from atop the foremast and with the sun at his back, a lookout can watch for the lighter shade of shallow water. In the afternoon, when the sun is ahead of the ship and its shine on the water obscures what is beneath the surface, the captain orders a new course away from the glare.

Eamon stands on the leeward side at the fore chains. The wind is light, the midday sun hot. *Atalanta* sails as close to the wind as she can, hoping to get around a chain of islands close by. With one hand, he swings the lead line to-and-fro over the water until he can circle it forward and let it go. As the lead sinks, the string feeds rapidly off the coil in his other hand. He counts the knots that go through his fingers. "One, two, three, four, five, six, seven . . ." The line stops feeding out when the lead hits the bottom. He started with the second knot in hand. "Nine fathoms!" he calls out. He recoils the string as he retrieves the lead and then looks at the wax in a cavity at its base. "Sand," he reports, giving the wax a cursory wipe. Splash! "Seven fathoms! Sand and shell." Accustomed to these soundings, the crew hardly hears them until the depths grow shallow. At three fathoms, *Atalanta* will run aground.

Splash. "Five fathoms! Sand and shell."

"Standby to wear ship," the captain calls. The men are already in the rigging and ready on deck.

Splash. "Eight fathoms!"

"Hold fast!"

Splash. "Nine fathoms!"

Splash. "Ten, sir."

"Stand down! We're around. Ease your helm two points and trim for speed."

✳ ✳ ✳

As the self-appointed English teacher to the "Chinamen," Coop mistakes their bows not as cultural norms but as gestures of personal respect. After a few days, though, he realizes how careful they are to avoid disrespect and confrontation. When they nod and say, "Yes," it means only that they've heard him, not that they understand or agree. As he picks up a little Mandarin, Coop swears he imitates their inflections only to have them laugh at his attempts. "But I said it exactly as you said it." Then they attempt the same with English, and it's his turn to shake his head. "No, no, no . . ."

On the way south, each "Chinaman" tucks the long braid of his hair inside his shirt or ties it into a knot to keep it out of the way. Crossing the equator, they panic when the shellbacks chop off their queues. Coop struggles to understand and finally translates that if these men return to China without their braided hair, they may be mistaken for someone not of their dynasty and face execution.

A slow start to her voyage, it takes a month before *Atalanta* raises Sunda Strait. When the wind dies, the Strait proves elusive. It lies close ahead of her when the second watch goes below at midnight and is still there four hours later when they're back on deck. When the wind finally fills, they fetch beyond the grip of the current and sail close by smoldering Krakatoa.

"It looks like hell itself!" Coop shakes his head.

Eamon agrees. "I've seen illustrations but never thought I'd lay my own eyes on it."

"You would have to see this to believe it," Sam adds.

Inspired, Coop offers, "Maybe I'll get a volcano tattoo."

Mister Ames's fleet is an offspring of the recently closed Dutch East India Company. To do the most business, he tries to position his ships between geopolitical lines. With Britain and France at war, neutrality proves tricky. To England, it's bad enough that France aided the American Revolution; now she has sold the Louisiana territories to the United States to feed her war chest. All this when England hardly accepts the nascent United States as independent. She sees American sailors as former British subjects. Should the American experiment fail, they may be her subjects again. Allied with France against British expansion, Americans appear oblivious to French intentions in Europe and entitled to their own in North America.

Where does this leave *Atalanta* and her crew among the far-flung harbors that dot the Indian Ocean? Isolated ports depend on visiting ships, and ships, in turn, never know when they will need a safe harbor. The ports hoist the flag of whichever power has sway over them, and neutral ports welcome ships regardless of their colors. If a warship finds a prize in a neutral harbor and intends to take her, she waits to do so at sea.

Facing uncertain politics and the remnants of Madagascar's once famous piracy, Captain Rolinson's priority is to keep his options open. He flies whatever colors will cause the least trouble. Beyond this bare subterfuge, *Atalanta* carries provisions for sixty or more days at sea. Barring scurvy, she can cross five thousand nautical miles nonstop, but she's already been at sea a month. To top off her stores, the old man plots a course for the Keeling Islands, where they will find sea turtles, bird eggs, coconuts, and fresh water. These islands appeal because they are uninhabited and unclaimed, but it is much easier to sail past than to find them. Six hundred nautical miles from Sunda Strait, they rise five yards above sea level and cover five square miles. Forested with coconut palms, the trees are taller than the islands are high. On the sixth day out, birds are sighted. On lookout, Coop watches the horizon and calls out the aqua shade of the clouds off the starboard bow. The shallows within the coral edges of the atoll, lit by bright sunshine, reflect their color up into the sky, turning the undersides of passing clouds from gray to aqua blue. This will be their last sight of land for more than a month.

Day in, day out, bounded by an empty horizon, today looks

exactly like yesterday and, no doubt, like tomorrow. High in the rigging, Eamon pays witness. *There is a rhythm to crossing an ocean, a harmony with invisible elements, a synchrony with a pelagic heartbeat. The only constant is the distance to the horizon. Every point on that edge looks like every other point. Our course is lost save for the compass, but the compass is not the earth's magnetic field. The sails are not the wind. Waves inhabit the water, but they are not the water itself. They lift each crest, drop it, and move on. Even my own body, made of water, akin to the oceans . . . is it me, or am I a self, made visible by a body? Firmament above and depths below, this surface we cross is the waist of an hourglass. We sail through time more than space.*

CHAPTER 20

IF A SHIP sails west at four knots for four hours, she travels sixteen nautical miles due west. This is "dead reckoning." It's simple arithmetic. At the end of each watch, the officer on deck estimates the ship's speed and reports the compass heading. When a ship approaches shore and margins for error narrow, this is done at the chime of every hour. Eamon translates this information onto the captain's charts, but no ship's speed or course is steady or straight. Currents push a ship off her course and speed. The compass tells only where the ship's bow aims. It can't tell that a current from the south is pushing her course northward. So, the dead reckoned position is only a good guess. It's the captain's noon and twilight sights with a sextant that correct the guess and "fix" the ship's position on the chart.

Three weeks out from Keeling Islands, the skies cloud over. Without the sun, moon, and stars, the sextant is useless. When the barometer's needle plummets, Captain Rolinson calls all hands. "Sway down the royals, t'gallants, and their masts. Foul weather is comin' for us."

An upper mast, with yardarm rigging and sail, weighs a ton. Lowering it to the deck while being tossed about high above the sea is especially dangerous but will be worth the risk if the old man's forecast proves correct. The full crew works with a will and is done in half a day.

The next morning, an ugly cloud looms over the horizon. Its leading edge is sharp, dark, and low. Tendrils curl beneath it like claws. The captain orders a new course, but their foe follows. A few warning gusts come ahead. The wind in the rigging rises in volume and pitch. A curtain of rain covers *Atalanta*. Through its gray cast, what looks like a tornado emerges astern.

"Wear ship! To northwest," the captain calls.

Eamon is mesmerized by the approaching monster. There is a cloud of spray at its base. Water churns up its sides. He hears its roar even at a distance. Jack shakes him out of his trance. "It's a waterspout, Eamon. Come on, get to the braces!" Shocked into action, he hurries to follow, glancing over his shoulder as he goes.

Atalanta comes to her new course, the spout feints toward the ship, and the sails go aback. *Atalanta* is helpless before this thing. At the last, it veers away.

"Eamon," comes the captain's voice. "Note our course change in the log at seven bells."

As Eamon starts for the captain's quarters, the rain thins. He reaches the companionway hatch when he hears the second mate's call. "Captain!" Mister Strom points off the starboard beam and says no more. In the distance, a phalanx of clouds like the last one approaches. *Atalanta* turns to run from them.

"Double lash the hatches and boats on deck. The only sails set shall be the tops'ls with fore stays'l."

At the captain's desk, Eamon notes the course change. The captain arrives, towels himself off, and points to the chart. "This storm should be heading south. That puts us on the better side of it. We're off course but have no choice."

Eamon is used to rough weather by now, but he recalls the wreck they saw at the docks in Hong Kong and asks, "Is it a typhoon, sir?"

"Typhoon, hurricane, cyclone. Different names from different oceans, but they're the same thing."

Within the hour, sails reduced, the captain gathers his crew again. "Steel yourselves, men. This will be a battle. Until we're through, one-hour tricks at the helm, two men at a time. The only other men on deck will be an officer and a lookout on the foremast. The rest will keep the bilge pumps going."

As the weather worsens, the waves build fast. These are not the mountainous seas south of the Horn with long periods between them. These brutes are marshaled in a hurry, steepen fast, and pummel *Atalanta* close behind one another. Her motion becomes jarring and violent. Cook gives up the galley. He lashes a keg full of hard tack in place and another of salted meat for the crew to grab for themselves.

Two ropes loop over a spoke on the wheel to hold her course. The men tethered to the binnacle stand by to slip the lashings if a course change is called, but the power in *Atalanta*'s sails can overwhelm her helm. She feels almost beyond control.

The wind picks up so much spray into the air that the men on deck face downwind to get a decent breath. The lookout is high enough on the foremast to breathe more easily, but getting there is a gamble. The next lookout's mates stand by at the forecastle hatch to slide it open and slam it shut behind him. Sensing the roll of the ship and the last wave that covered the deck, timing it right, he can dash out the hatch and to the ratlines at the windward rail before the next wave catches him. If he makes it, he climbs fast. If he doesn't make it, the wave sweeps him off his feet and washes him into the bulwarks hard enough to break bones. Or worse, it might cast him overboard. Once he is "safely" on the fore topmast, he sends the man he relieves down and then hangs on for a hell of a ride. An hour feels like two before the next lookout slaps him on the back and sends him through the obstacle course in reverse. All this when visibility is often reduced to zero and keeping a lookout seems pointless.

With nightfall, their world turns pitch-black. The wind screeching in rigging reaches a maniacal tone. Deep in the belly of the storm, the continuous shriek is unnerving. It threatens to drive you raving mad. Covering your ears doesn't help. Some of the men scream back, only proving how small and unheard they are. Still, they scream.

Sleep is impossible. Hammocks swing wildly. Each man tries to brace himself somewhere and close his eyes, but his muscles keep clenching with every lurch and shudder of the ship. Eight men at a time, in the darkest belly of the ship and waist-deep in water, work the two big bilge pumps to exhaustion until their mates take over for them. Chips checks often to see if the water is gaining on them or they on it.

Atalanta charges on, blind. So far, damages and injuries are minor. All the men can do is hold on. And pump. The captain curses the barometer. "Damn you, stop dropping!" In the morning, his curse is granted, and its needle starts to rise. He sends Cook to bear good news to the men.

At that moment, for his turn at lookout, Sam hangs on halfway up the foremast. The riot that surrounds him is madness until, *What's that?* Another curtain of rain obscures his view. Does he hear something? The rain thins. To leeward, maybe a mile off, he catches sight, loses sight, and then clearly sees a white line of breaking waves booming on a reef. They extend north and south as far as he can see. There is no landmass beyond them. He almost chokes as he bellows for all he is worth, "Breakers! BREAKERS! It's a reef! We're heading for a reef!"

Moses is at the helm. Before he hears Sam's hysteria, he wonders what it is he feels through the soles of his feet. He tilts his head to listen and squints to leeward while resting a hand on the wheel. When Sam's call comes, he doesn't need to discern the words. Before Spanky or Mister Strom can react, he slips the loops from the wheel's spoke and lets the ship come up to starboard, almost laying her abeam to the seas. She rolls heavily, as if to turn over.

The crew below feels the sudden change, and *Atalanta* is not standing back up. Fear in each other's eyes, they rush for the companionway. On deck, they hear a new voice. It's Moses shouting to Sam, "LOOK FOR A GAP, MAN! A GAP!" Jack grips the windward rail and relays the plea to Sam. Despite the impossible maelstrom, Jack's call sparks hope in Sam. In his mind, the plea becomes fact. *There could be a gap? There* has to *be a gap! Where is it?*

Captain Rolinson comes up on the quarter deck. He sees that Moses somehow owns the helm and with it holds *Atalanta* in his hands. When he reaches the wheel, their eyes meet. Moses shouts above the storm, "We must heave to, sir. Buy some time."

These words are almost defiant, but the captain hears their truth and calls, "Drop the jibs and back the main top." *Atalanta* can't lay across the seas for long, though. Inevitably, she will either drift onto the reef or broach and be overwhelmed before she strikes.

But now Sam calls, "THERE! THERE IT IS! TO LARBOARD! THERE'S A GAP! HARD TO LARBOARD!"

The captain and Moses force the wheel to port. The jib is rehoisted and main top filled. As *Atalanta* turns, she stands back up and jibes. She gains steerage and charges toward the gap in the breakers. It looks like suicide, but breakers are everywhere else. Everyone grips something solid and holds their breath, desperate for enough depth to sail through.

The men feel the impact as if it tears their own skins. Thrown forward, some of them fall. They hear splintering. Some rigging goes slack. *Atalanta* shudders to a stop with white water crashing on either side. Moses and the captain are thrown from the wheel. Her bowsprit is above deeper water where there are only whitecaps. She is so close to making it through the gap and over the reef! The next wave meets her transom as if it were hitting a cliff, sending spray high into the wind, bursting the windows in the captain's cabin, and tearing the rudder from the ship. As the wave rolls under her, she jolts forward.

The captain's first order is to Moses. "Drop the anchor and let the rode run. If we get over this afloat, make it fast. I don't want to get pushed into more shallows beyond." Moses gathers men and runs forward. The next order is to the mates. "Set the fore and main courses. They might carry her over."

When the next wave jars *Atalanta*, it is the last straw for the fore topmast. There is a loud cracking, tearing sound as it carries over the side, taking the jibboom with it. Coop and Eamon catch each other's eyes. "Sam!" They stumble down the slanting deck to the leeward rail and scan the water for their friend. The shattered spars, twisted rigging, and upper topsail are a confused wreckage on choppy water in the lee of the ship's hull.

"Where is he? Sam!" Coop calls. He and Eamon pull on lines from this mass, but it surges away, almost pulling them overboard before it batters back into the hull.

"He can't swim!" Eamon cries.

Coop knows it, too, and gets ready to dive in before Jack grabs him. "Don't be a fool! He's drowned and ya will be too." He drags Coop to join the men sheeting home the nearest sail. Eamon can't move. He thinks, *When did I stop breathing?* and gasps. Jack leaves him where he stands. Chips and the bosun arrive with axes to cut the fallen rigging away.

As the courses fill, they snap taut, and *Atalanta* heels more. The crew feels her lift on the next wave, move a few yards, and pound back down. Another sail. Another wave. She moves painfully, but she moves. At Mister Duncan's warning, the men look aft to see a wave bigger than the rest. If it doesn't lift *Atalanta*, it will bury her. When it strikes, a jagged spasm shakes the ship. The stern slews to port. Men are washed into the bulwarks or overboard. A backwash returns one of them aboard. It's a disaster, but the ship is afloat. Not on her lines, but not aground and not sunk. Not yet.

"Moses," the captain calls, "give the anchor a shot of rode. Chips! Take men to the pumps and report back. Mates! Strike all sail."

Sails struck, anchor holding, *Atalanta*'s battered bow points into the wind and the gap she struggled through. Gigantic surf breaks on the outside of the reef. The men thank their luck to be on the inside, but the reef gives no relief from the wind. *Atalanta* still shudders in the gusts. The wreckage from the fore topmast is tethered astern. The crew manages to rig a heavy sail under her hull to cover the worst damage. She's low in the water. Chips does what he can to patch the hull from the inside while the men exhaust themselves pumping the bilge. Otherwise, they collapse and listen to the surf detonate on the reef all night.

CHAPTER 21

BY SUNRISE, THE wind relents. The waves will take longer to calm down. Daylight reveals *Atalanta* surrounded by cloudy shallows. From the top of the mainmast, Captain Rolinson estimates the reef is two miles wide. It stretches north nine or ten miles and south as far as the eye can see. There is an island nearby and a dozen others widely dispersed. All are small. Half of them support foliage and the larger ones sustain coconut palms.

On the nearest beach are two bodies. Four men are missing.

Back on deck, the captain calls all hands. "We've come to grief, but we're not a wreck yet. We shipped spare timber, cordage, and sailcloth in Hong Kong and can salvage the foretop for its rigging. We will careen as soon as we are able. Chips will make what repairs he can. Without a rudder, we'll rig a sweep astern and steer with sail trim. To get out of these shallows, we must lighten ship. So, we'll shuttle to shore what we can of the cargo and our provisions and make camp there. Then we'll find a channel and pull her around to clear water. Once we reload, we'll make way. It's hard work ahead, but there's no other way to reach the nearest port." He pauses. "First, let us bury the dead."

Sick at the loss of his friend, Eamon is compelled to see if one of the dead bodies is Sam's. He, Coop, Jack, and half the crew volunteer for the burials. The others remain aboard to sort out the wreckage and continue pumping the bilge. The captain stays aboard to study his charts and outline their escape. He puts Mister Strom in charge of the shore party and hands him the ship's Bible.

There *is* a vast distance between a captain and his crew. Every detail and consequence traces to him. What crew did he choose? What ship? Did he take proper care of her? Of the cargo and their itinerary? In the face of forces beyond his control, there are two constants that define a captain's options: was the voyage profitable and was it fast? Meeting these two criteria earns the respect of a captain's employer and crew. Without either of these, he will lose his command.

Instead of pushing through the storm, Captain Rolinson could have hove *Atalanta* to. But heaving to is slow. Even "cowardly," his crew might judge. "Hard driving" captains never give up sailing their ship. Anything less than sailing is doomed. Heaving to might have left *Atalanta* on the worse side of the cyclone, and no one knows if she would have survived that. She fought hard enough on the better side. So, the crew doesn't blame Captain Rolinson for their trouble. Still, he knows credit and blame are his alone.

Sam's is not one of the bodies on the beach. One is Tommy, the other Will'm. The fourth missing man is Gates, the bosun.

"They must've floated out to sea," Jack guesses.

"Maybe he's a dolphin now." Coop wants to believe.

Shovel in hand, Eamon cannot find his voice.

Swede finishes stitching a sailcloth bag around Tommy and does the same for Will'm. The men carry the bodies to the island's highest point and dig below a palm tree. It's quick work in sandy soil. After they're done and the second mate reads a passage from the Bible, they look around and take some time to themselves. Where they are is *not* a bad place. In fact, it's beautiful, but the men are numb and not yet able to see it.

Back aboard ship, Jack is promoted to bosun and starts a few men salvaging the wreckage of the fore topmast. They find Sam's body tangled up in its lines and sails. "Spanky, go get Eamon and Coop. I'll tell Swede we need another shroud."

At some point, Sam had doctored every member of the crew. They are sad to lose him, especially the men who need him now. To a man, they sing some praise of him. Not the least of which that he saved their lives when he was the lookout.

"At least we'll bury him on shore." Coop consoles himself.

"Aye. He'd have hated a watery grave," Eamon agrees.

"You're right." Jack pauses and then looks up. "We been thrown together long enough, I was startin' to think I could keep you three alive."

"You almost did. For more than a year now, but there was nothing you could do."

Jack shakes his head and shrugs. "Let's get this over with."

Spanky helps them to lower the body into a longboat and row ashore. There, they find Cook in charge of making camp. When they tell him it's Sam's body they carry, he stops bossing everyone and helps them. After burying Sam, one by one, they go back to work. Coop leaves Eamon for last but turns to listen when he hears him talking. "I regret we couldn't do better for you, Sam. You did well for us, you old mule." There is a long pause. "It's not a bad view, though, and you're not alone. Tommy and Will'm are close by. I'll tell your family about you and about this place, and I'll be back before we go." Eamon visits Sam's grave at sunset most days after.

It takes a week for the bay where *Atalanta* swings at anchor to turn from turbid to crystalline, revealing a colorful coral ecosystem. There are countless schools of fish, large coconut crabs, and big sea turtles. Every day, one of the mates is assigned a detail of a few men to take a gig and survey for a way out of the atoll. As long as they are not working aboard the ship or at the camp, they fish and hunt for the evening meal. Not knowing how long they will be stranded, it's necessary to augment their stores. They are surprised to find goats and pigs on the bigger islands, evidence of the livestock left by past shipwrecks and fishermen. The meat from these is a welcome change from seafood stew. There are thousands of birds on the islands too. The men raid the nests for eggs and sometimes catch the birds. The fowl is no more than edible.

The camp is Cook's kingdom, and he rules it from a tent set up as his galley. With limited fresh water, Swede patches together sailcloth and barrels to catch rain from the near daily thunderstorms. Most of the crew hang their hammocks on the island between trees or lay them on the sand. The captain only sleeps in his own tent ashore when *Atalanta* is careened. Since they are not underway and no one stands watch, everyone sleeps through the night and works all day.

Surveying and harvesting are the most desired duties on any given day. These give the men a break from the ship and the rest of the crew. Instead of rowing loads of cargo and provisions ashore and repairing and rerigging the ship, they fashion nets, spears, and fishhooks to go hunting and exploring. Moses must have been a fisherman before he was a sailor. He teaches the others how to improvise their tools and catches twice as much as anyone else. The men feel like little kids on these forays, surprised to hear their own laughter. They define their calendar by their turn to go roaming. One party sails and rows to the most promising island at the south end of the reef and camps there for the night.

After three weeks, Eamon is putting the finishing touches on a new chart when the captain calls the mates and Jack to his cabin. "I believe we're stranded on Cargados Carajos. If there are other charts of this place, they would be sketches by the fishermen who come here. With luck, one of them might arrive and take word of our plight to Isle de France, but I'll not wait for rescue. Looking this over, is there anything you see from your surveys that we've left out?"

Mister Duncan studies the chart. "Sir, I'm sure I mentioned the wreck we found about halfway to that southern tip. Six or seven hundred ton, Arab, I'm guessing, from her coir cables."

"You did. Point to it and Eamon will mark its ribs. Mister Strom, you noted signs of a fishing camp on this northern island?"

"Yes, sir. What you've got there looks correct."

"Very well. We've patched the hull the best we can and emptied her. She's high in the water. In fact, I'd rather have her ballasted, but she draws less now, and the longboats can tow her better as she is." He looks up. "We can't get out of this lagoon the way we came in. It was the storm's surge that lifted her and pushed us through. Hell, half the islands we see now were under water then. They're little more than sandbanks. Your soundings, though, show two channels north of us. The nearer one is too narrow. The farther is four miles off. You've found five and eight fathoms on the way there. The nights have been calm, so we'll likely move at night."

Mister Strom waits to speak in deference to Mister Duncan. "Sir, we've also found a lot of coral heads. They're all over the place. Especially a band of them about a mile away. There." He points. "We'd be hard-pressed to find a way through in daylight."

"That's well and good if we get a calm day, but Chips and Coop are making floats for you. With twine and weights, you'll anchor the floats on the particular coral heads that will be to either side of us as we go. If we can get through that patch, we can get out. I want a channel marked even if we move in daylight."

"And if we run aground, sir?"

"We'll only move on a rising tide. She'll suffer if she grounds, but your job is to mark a channel so she'll not come to that. Rowing her out might take more than one attempt. If we must, we'll anchor a hundred yards at a time. Once we escape the middle of the reef, we can sail the ten miles to anchor in its lee. We've jury-rigged the fore topmast. The main course, top, and stays'ls will drive us. The jibs, fore course, and top will steer us down. With the sweep, the spanker will bear us up. And with no ballast, we'll not use the upper sails. I want to reload at the new anchorage as soon as possible. If any of the men pray, tell them to ask for a following wind. At best, we can only hope to broad reach. Isle de France is two hundred and fifty miles south. If we miss it, we will end up on the shores of Madagascar or Africa. If we make it, we can finish repairs there and carry on." This sounded ominous but almost plausible. "You mates will take a longboat and four men each. Take the best swimmers with you.

Report back when you finish or at dusk. You're all dismissed."

The following day, the old man commandeers a longboat. Vasco, Toren, Axel, and Coop row while the second mate gives a tour of their proposed exit from the reef. The oars knock a rhythm between their tholepins as Mister Strom goes into detail. "There are six legs to it, sir. If we post signal fires, we'll not need the moonlight. We'll know what bearings to keep them on and when to make each turn. Men posted at the fires will wait until they hear our cannon to light them."

The captain nods. "Even with clear skies and daylight, I'd want the fires."

"Aye, sir. This is the crowded patch here. We'll turn to leg two as soon as we see the fire on this beach to larboard. Then we'll keep it on our stern for a hundred yards. We'll turn when the third and fourth fires line up as a range. The last fire is at the pass. When it bears north of us, we'll turn for it."

"What about current? Is there enough to sweep us off our lines?"

"Not here, sir, but it's considerable at the pass. It will sweep us out, but we'll be making sail by then."

"If it goes wrong here, at least it will do so gently. Good work, Mister Strom."

"Thank you, sir."

The rest of the day, the crew can only wait. Wait and gather the strength they'll need to weigh anchor and tow the ship through the maze of shallows and corals. There's too much wind to move the ship the first night, and the men resume their chores the next day. That night, when the sun drops, the wind goes with it. They're ready, and the cannon is fired.

"Touch and go" on leg two and three, *Atalanta* stops when she grounds but only for a moment. The men pull harder on the longboats' oars to tow her free. It's a brutal night's work. At dawn, she clears her exit from the reef and sails to anchor in the lee of the archipelago. The men are weary, but it's a victory, and they start believing they can save themselves. Closer to their escape, the captain drives them harder. Rowing the miles back and forth from dawn to dusk between the ship and their island, it takes five days to break down camp and load cargo. On the day they finish, the captain grants them grog and a "Sunday meal." He will relent until dawn to weigh anchor and make sail, so the men break out a fiddle, penny whistle, and drum to sing and dance on the foredeck. With the captain's consent, Eamon and Coop row back to visit their friend's grave for the last time. The music and voices follow them over calm water.

Eamon has grown used to talking to dead Sam. "This is it, Sam. Tomorrow, we'll weigh anchor and be off. We're here to say goodbye. We all must someday, I suppose." He pauses. "The sun's droppin'. It's a little egg-shaped, so close to the horizon and ripples, like it's liquid." Eamon waits. "Molten now, like it's pouring into the sea. So calm, I can hear the men on deck." The other sounds are the lap of ripples on the shore and a sparse chatter from birds in their nests. The sky is empty. "There, 'tis gone, Sam." He watches a while. "The clouds in the west look afire. To the east, stars are starting out. It all reflects off the sea like a looking glass. I wish you could see it. I . . ." He sighs. "We'll not forget you, Sam, and you'll be missed by more."

Uncomfortable, Coop wants to say anything to stave off tears. "I wish you could see it too." He turns to Eamon. "Maybe this sky ablaze is him sayin' goodbye to us."

"I hope so, Coop. Let's remember it. And him. Goodbye, Sam."

They push off the beach to row back. As the colors darken, the skiff's bow cleaves a surface that looks almost bloodred while, in its wake, stars pinpoint their twins onto an indigo mirror. A mournful tune from the penny whistle ripples across the water. The other sound is wood on wood as the oars knock back and forth. Fully dark when they get back, Jack catches their lines. The whistle's tune finished is followed by a hush. Most of the men find somewhere on deck to sleep.

CHAPTER 22

ATALANTA SAILS FOUR days before she swings at anchor in the shelter of Grand Bay, Isle de France. Several other vessels are there, none of them quite her size. Two are navy frigates flying British colors. Several smaller vessels ply in and out of the bay, to and from the beach and to several piers that extend from a busy village. Beyond this, cultivated fields fit together like puzzle pieces. Their patchwork leads to lush green foothills before a spine of rugged peaks in the distance. In the bright sun, shadows of small puffy clouds move west across the almost sparkling landscape.

Sailors' eyes are always thirsty for the next landfall. Every member of the crew is on deck, gaping at the island like a long-lost lover. They have made it to her embrace. They breathe her in. It will take time to forget that they might have breathed their last recently. Eamon overhears, "It's so green," "Ain't it beautiful," and "Sight for sore eyes, it is," muttered around the deck.

Atalanta is a different sort of sight. Her fore topmast is new. Her fore topgallant and royal masts, along with their sails, are absent. Her bowsprit is jury-rigged and shortened. Some upper yards are bare of sail. She has obviously suffered.

"Isle de France," the captain says to himself, "and two British frigates in harbor? Bosun! I'll take a longboat and four men to shore. Mister Duncan, the rest of you will remain aboard. You'll all have your leave tonight. If any officers come to call, they will be welcome when I return."

Jack chooses Moses, Coop, and Johnny for his crew. The old man steers toward the longest pier. Locals, most of them African, help pull the boat up on the sand. They smile their welcome and speak a patois that leaves the captain confused.

"It's Creole, sir," Moses volunteers. "I can translate for you."

He studies Moses. "Very well. Ask them where I can find the harbormaster."

A moment later, he says, "This man says you can follow him there."

"Very good. You three stay with the boat. Moses, fall in behind me." As they walk, the captain asks over his shoulder, "How is it that you know Creole?"

"I grew up on this island, sir."

This stops the captain's stride. He turns to face Moses but says nothing.

"Yes, sir. Until I was ten. My grandmother died then, and I stowed away on a ship. It's a long story. I never belonged here. I'm not White, and all the Africans I saw were slaves. I didn't want to be a slave, so I left. Still, I know this place and these people. Or I did. The people I knew may still be in Port Louis. That's where you'll find the shipyard *Atalanta* needs, ten more miles down the coast."

The captain shakes his head. "If you did not belong here, where did you come from?"

"I was born a castaway, sir. My ancestors were from Madagascar, en route to slavery here when their ship wrecked on a desert island. A hundred of them died, and sixty made it to shore, but the island was barren. Their conditions were worse than those we just left. The island is only two weeks west of here, but it took fifteen years before we were rescued. Seven women and me not yet walking. We were all that was left. When we got here, the governor took pity, declared us free, and gave us new names. Thirty and five years ago."

"Remarkable. If I hadn't heard of the wreck, I wouldn't believe you. What was its name?"

"The wreck? Utile, sir."

"And the island?"

"It was the Isle of Sand. Now it is named Tromelin, after our rescuer."

"And his ship?"

"The Dauphine, sir. My grandmother was named after her."

"So, you are the end of that story."

"Unless some half brother or sister walks on this island. My mother disappeared into the midst of the islanders. I don't remember her."

"It seems being shipwrecked follows you."

"I hope not, sir."

"Me as well. So, you knew this island as French."

"Yes, sir."

"Yet we have British warships in harbor. Let's see what we shall find. I may need your local knowledge to get us out of here."

"Sir, are you promoting me?"

"That will be of no matter unless I still have a ship."

Captain Rolinson learns from the harbormaster that the island was won by the British a few months ago to stop French corsairs raiding from here. Otherwise, the only change they've made is reverting the island's name to Mauritius. They have no interest in displacing residents and don't want to upset the sugarcane economy so long as they can tax it. The captain realizes his hope to make repairs and carry on is thin. Finally, he asks where he can find a doctor for three of his men injured during the cyclone. He, too, misses Sam.

As soon as they return to *Atalanta*, a longboat approaches from one of the navy frigates. At the boat's bow is an officer in uniform. Captain Rolinson rarely stands on ceremony, and what food is left aboard is not fit to serve. He decants some rum and selects two goblets before going to welcome their visitor.

"I am Captain Rolinson, sir. Welcome aboard *Atalanta*, or what's left of her."

The contrast between the two men is stark. The Brit looks half the old man's age. His black coat's two rows of buttons shine bright, his white trousers are spotless and creased, and his shoes are polished.

Behind him, two marines, in clean red and white uniforms, stand at attention, each with a musket topped by a bayonet. He removes his bicorn, tucks it under his left arm, and puts his right arm behind his back. With a crisp tilt of his head, he reports, "Captain Parker, sir, at your service." Despite his official bearing, he breaks into a smile. "What's left of her indeed. You'll have a story to tell, but first, sir, your alliance? Your colors are new to me: a gold triangle edged with red waves?"

"And new to me, as well. Our flag is improvised from a Chinese dynasty. We sailed under American colors since launching a decade ago but were sold to a company out of Hong Kong last year. Her new owners were part of the Dutch East India Company until it closed. They're independent now and neutral. We loaded their cargo, and they doubled our crew."

Parker considers *Atalanta*'s ragged crew with sympathy. "Will you be limping back to Hong Kong then?"

"Not if I can make repairs, sir. I believe there's a shipyard nearby, and I have need of a rudder. After that, my orders are to trade at large. Perhaps tea for sugar here."

"Of course, you have this year's tea!" Captain Parker's enthusiasm is obvious. "And yes, there's a yard that could fit a rudder for you. In Port Louis."

"Captain," Rolinson nods, saying, "we tried to save what we could of our cargo when we stranded. Perhaps you would sample some and give me your opinion?" It is a thinly disguised invitation, but he hopes it is enough to open the door for the bribes he expects to pay. Cook hurries to boil some water, and soon the old man is telling Parker of the cyclone over tea.

When Captain Parker debarks, Rolinson gives the crew their leave. Mister Duncan posts a schedule of short watches. Everyone will work during the day, as usual. At night, the men will be on four at a time for two hours, to pump the bilge and stand anchor watch. They'll have some nights off entirely. The captain hopes his generosity will keep their loyalty while he gets his bearings and makes a plan.

If Eamon doesn't count going to Mingzhu, this is his first shore leave since Buenos Aires. Surprised to find himself stretching his legs around town with the rest of the crew, it dawns on him that the captain understands he will not jump ship so long as *Atalanta* sails toward the American states. Eamon shakes his head and laughs to himself. He has forgotten what being at his leisure is like. Every sight, sound, and smell is refreshed by newfound freedom. Unable to spend his wages until now, he has enough money to buy the first round of drinks. Due on watch at midnight, he has no need for an inn but looks forward to a decent meal ashore. Out of habit, he thinks to send a letter home but realizes he might well arrive before it. It would have borne sad news, anyway, news he can't imagine writing and sending.

"Where you blokes from?" A young British sailor from one of the navy frigates stands at the bar with them, mug of beer in hand.

"We sailed from Hong Kong," Coop answers. "Ten weeks ago."

"Ten weeks? Your ship looks faster than that, though she's worse for wear."

"We were caught by a cyclone almost a month ago and stranded on a reef. Three days north of here."

"St. Brandon's, we call it. How did you survive that?"

Eamon leaves Coop to embellish their exploits. In another pub, he finds a table in a corner. Halfway through savoring his lamb pot pie and beer, he eavesdrops on a conversation between a marine and midshipman at the next table.

"She's a mess, she is. Our ships may be battle scarred, but she's worse than we are. Her rudder's gone!"

"It *was* a hell of a storm."

"Her lines look fast, though. Give her a few weeks in the yard, and she'd be a fine prize without a shot fired."

"No one would ransom her if she has no alliance."

"If her cargo's any good, selling it would pay for arming her . . ."

Alarmed at this, Eamon is confused by his feelings. *After all,* he thinks, Atalanta is *my home. If she's taken, how will I get back? Would the Brits press us into his majesty's service? Can I find another ship? Where are ships bound from here? England? Could I get home from England?*

Something next is coming. This is his chance to take a breath and face whatever it will be. He orders bread pudding and a glass of port.

As he pays his bill and rises to leave, Eamon senses being watched. He turns, scans the noisy room, and sees Mister Duncan with Paddy and Rye at the bar. The mate stares at him, chuffs a smirk, and downs his drink. Eamon continues to head for the door. Once outside, he walks quickly up the dark, empty street. Behind him, he hears the door open. He doesn't want to look, but he needs to know. He pauses to see the light that spills from the pub door and the shadow from which the mate steps.

"What's your hurry, Eamon?"

Eamon turns and runs.

"You're not on watch until midnight!" the mate shouts after him and follows at a walk. Paddy and Rye join him, and he motions them toward other streets.

After running a few blocks and random turns, Eamon is lost. *Horrors! Where am I? Where's the pub? I'm safer in a crowd. I could go back and find a few mates.* As he turns one corner, he sees someone ahead. The silhouette tells him it's not the mate, but is it Paddy or Rye? He flattens himself into a doorway and waits. *Damnit, Sam, where are you when I need you?* The figure from the distance walks by not seeing him and not looking for him. Breathing again, Eamon reasons, *Maybe he came from an inn,* and goes that direction. When he turns the next corner, he finds an alley and the reek of urine. *Damn! I could shout for help, but what if it's the mate who answers?* Eamon hurries to the end of the alley, peeks up and down the street, and walks quickly on. *Downhill. That will get me back to the waterfront and a pub.* He tacks between buildings and catches glimpses of the bay. Rushing around another corner, he bowls Rye right over.

"Ho!" Rye shouts from the ground and grabs one of Eamon's ankles. "I have him! He's here!"

Eamon falls hard but kicks and Rye loses his grip. In an instant, Eamon is on his feet and running. Fear pushes Eamon faster than hostility does Rye. After turning a few corners, he no longer hears pursuit and ducks into another alley. Hands on knees, Eamon tries to catch and quiet his breath. He's nauseous. When he can stand, he clutches both sides of his head, desperate, and looks around. The alley is wide and ends at two doors. Above them is a sign: "Blacksmith." *A weapon! That's what I need.* A pile of firewood meant for the forge is there. He rummages through it and finds a stout piece of limb, three feet long. "Not a blade," he whispers, "but it will answer." Bolstered but still wary, he starts down the street.

When he stands in the shadows of the buildings bordering the shore, Eamon looks across the beach to the pier. The longboat will drop off and pick up crew there. *Too exposed,* he thinks. *It's wide open from here to there, and someone could watch for me from the shadow of the pier. Maybe I could run when the boat approaches or swim to it.*

The sound of voices and music draws him back into the maze that is the town. When he turns what he hopes will be the last corner to the safety of numbers, he sees the mate coming. Eamon backs into the nearest shadow, raises his weapon, and holds his breath. As the mate stalks past, Eamon can easily strike him. He musters all his strength.

A door bursts open from the end of the street behind the mate. Light and cacophony pour out along with four patrons. Eamon drops his club and runs toward the men. "Ahoy!" he shouts. As he nears them, he realizes they're Brits and adds, "God save the King!" before ducking inside.

Startled when the club hits the ground, Mister Duncan turns to see Eamon's retreat. *Damn! How did I miss him?* Then, *Why didn't he hit me?* and when he feels the heft of the club, he's confused. *He could have laid me low with this.*

❊ ❊ ❊

Once aboard *Atalanta*, Eamon seeks out the captain.

"Of course, they'll want to claim her for their own. She'd be a fine warship," Rolinson answers. "Appears we've sailed into a trap."

"Can they do that, sir?"

"Not without arguing their claim before a prize court. For that, they'll place officers and a cadre of marines in command and have us sail her to Cape Town. Likely, that's the nearest court. Three weeks away. Maybe four. Without legitimizing their claim, taking her would be piracy."

"Wouldn't it be a British court, sir?"

"It would be biased, certainly, but I can argue our neutrality. Failing that, they would judge the value of *Atalanta* and her cargo and award shares to the captain and crew who claim her as their prize."

"What about us, her crew? Would they press us into their navy?"

"The court doesn't expect captured men to be loyal. Under a flag of truce, they may return crewmen to their own country."

"To the United States?" Eamon can't hide hope from his voice.

"Not when we sail from Hong Kong."

"Oh, no!"

"Or they would ship us to a neutral country and leave us to make our own way."

"Can you convince a court to let *Atalanta* go?"

"Our best chance may not be the court. Instead, it might be bribing the island's new governor. A prize court won't award him anything, but I will."

Without a ship and crew to command, a captain is no one. Like surviving the sale of the ship, the cyclone, and the stranding, Rolinson will continue to do any and everything to keep his command. With too many questions and not enough answers, he focuses on one task at a time, and this moment's task is to replace the rudder.

At dawn, the captain and Moses wave down a horse-drawn cart

to go overland to Port Louis. They plan to contract with the yard for materials and labor and return to *Atalanta* the next day. Whereupon they will sail to Port Louis at their first chance. Moses shakes his head as they roll past small hamlets and pastoral scenes.

"Has this place changed so much, Moses?"

"No, sir. It's not the place. It looks much as I left it. It's time that's confusing me. The further we go, the more I feel like the child I was."

"Of course. What will you do after we conduct our business?"

"I suppose I'll visit the intendant's house, where I lived in the servants' quarters. I'll look for anyone I knew."

"Where will you room tonight?"

"More than a room, I may need a stiff drink, sir."

"Very well. You can spend your per diem however you choose. We'll find an inn for me. Be sure to meet me there by the morning watch."

As their cart enters the outskirts of Port Louis, they pass a large construction site. Asking the man driving the cart, Moses relays, "It's a racetrack, sir. For horses." Before arriving at the shipyard, he points to a market. "Cook will want to provision there."

The captain is surprised by how the shipyard has already surmised much about *Atalanta*. They have cleared their ways and organized the timber for a new rudder, spars, and hull planks. Their foundry stands by to forge what *Atalanta* will need, and they give the captain and Moses a tour of the sail loft.

"Will you require more cordage, sir?" one of the riggers asks.

"No, we were able to salvage our rigging. We could use sail cloth, though, if you have spares." He pauses. "I am impressed by your preparations. Were you told to expect us?"

"Rumors travel fast on an island, sir."

This does not satisfy the captain's unasked question, so he's out with it point-blank. "Are we making repairs for ourselves or for the British navy?"

"As I said, sir, it's only a rumor."

"Aye, it is. But we are not an enemy ship nor is our cargo contraband. By rights, they may have a hard time convincing a prize court."

"In any case, sir, we're here to build and repair ships, and that includes yours."

❊ ❊ ❊

It is dusk when Moses weaves a drunken path to let himself through the back gate onto the grounds of the house where he grew up. His own body and breath feel surreal to him. The coiffed gardens and lawns look as he remembers them. He makes his way to the servant's cabins, feeling ten years old again. So much so that when he comes upon an ancient man standing at a workbench, his vantage from a head taller than the old man is a shock. Childhood Moses remembers this man as big and tall.

Softly, he bids, "*Bonswa tonton.*"

The old man looks up from sharpening a hand scythe. His short white hair contrasts with the deeply lined black face it surrounds. In a heartbeat his expression goes from benevolence to confusion to wide-eyed disbelief. His hand covers his mouth and then drops to grip his chest. "*Se li ou?*"

"Yes, Uncle, it is me."

"Moses . . ." The old man squeezes his eyes shut and opens them to see if the sight before him is still there. They are damp now. Standing back, his smile shows bright white teeth. "*Se vréman ou? Gade ou!*"

"Yes, really me. And look at you! I did not believe I would ever see you again."

"Oh! *Vini,*" he says, whereupon he joins Moses in English, "come, don't say another word until Auntie is with us."

"I thought I would find her first, or Rose, but here you are."

"Yes, I am here. Forever here." He shakes his head. "But Rose, she is gone."

"Gone?" Some intuition braces him for the answer. "Where?"

"*Li te mouri.*" Uncle shakes his head."

"Oh, Uncle, I am saddened for you."

"*Vini, vini.* Come. Let us hope the shock of seeing you doesn't send Auntie to join her." The old man pats Moses's shoulder tentatively at first and then harder. "Come. She will have something for us to eat."

Of course, they find Auntie in the kitchen. They can hear her humming a tune as they approach. Uncle pauses at the door, spreads a hand on Moses's chest, and holds a finger to his lips before going in. "*Tante, mwen gen yon sipriz pou ou.*" (Auntie, I have a surprise for you.) When she looks up from the dough she kneads, he is quick to clarify, "*Yon bon sipriz.*" (A good surprise.) "*Men gen fos.*" (But be strong.) She frowns at him now.

Moses steps into the kitchen and she gasps. "*Bonswa tante.*" After a moment, he adds, "Respire!"

She wipes her hands on her apron as she pushes past Uncle. At first, she holds Moses at arm's length and studies him. Not knowing whether to laugh or cry, she hugs him. They soon sit at the kitchen table, eating biscuits, sipping beer, and catching up on twenty-five years.

CHAPTER 23

WHILE THE CAPTAIN and Moses are away, the rest of the crew's attention is captured when ten or so boats sail together back and forth in the harbor. A crowd is growing at the end of each pier. *Atalanta's* crew watches from the railing, and Jack calls to Eamon, "Scribe! Can ya spare a page and pen from the captain's desk?"

"What's this?"

"Looks like a race is about to start, and there are some gamblers among us. If ya record the bets, I'll hold the purse, and we'll have some fun." As Eamon heads below for Jack's request, he hears him calling, "Gentlemen, gentlemen!" By the time he returns, the crew is studying the gathering fleet and choosing where to place their bets while the second mate lowers their best gig into the water to join the race. Coop, Swede, Toren, and Spanky are ready to crew for him.

"Mister Strom, sir," Jack calls. "Shall we let the other boats know that we have a purse here and the winner will have half of it?"

The second mate nods. "Aye, Jack. That should make things interesting."

"Then we'll split the rest between whoever picks the winner."

"Very well. I'll put five shillings on our own boat."

"That's bold, sir. Well done. If ya win the race, you'll have the whole prize unless some of us bet on ya too. What do ya say, mates?"

The men are busy sizing up the fleet. Eamon tries to understand each man's description of his chosen boat, but they keep coming back to change their choice. When he looks up, he realizes why: twice as many boats as before joust about near an apparent starting line. There is a glint in Jack's eyes. "I believe word of our prize money got out."

"It's that low-slung schooner with two raked masts." Cook explains his wager to Eamon.

The starting line runs from the end of the long pier to a rowboat anchored thirty yards off. Following where the men point, Eamon sees another boat anchored out near the mouth of the harbor and a third in the middle of the bay. A man in each of them has a flag in hand. Racing around the harbor, part of the course will include dodging the ships and boats at anchor. Being one of them, *Atalanta* will have front row seats for the race.

More boats launch from the beach, and a longboat rows to *Atalanta* from Captain Parker's frigate. She draws close by, and the officer at her helm calls, "Ahoy, *Atalanta*. We have ten pounds sterling that says our longboat will beat your gig to the finish."

"Whoa!" Jack answers. "What is the course, and where might that finish be?"

"The race will be twice 'round, leaving the marks to larboard. Our ship will strike her bell and hoist a pennant five minutes before firing a cannon for the start."

Jack looks at the breeze. "Are the boats to sail *and* row?"

"There are no rules. Whichever boat gets 'round first wins, but we're not betting we will win, only that our boat will beat yours."

"Stand by." Jack turns to his mates. "What say men? 'Tis a bit rich for us, but if we each pitch in four shillings, we'd have five pounds on the line." This is met with grumbling and remarks about the size of the Brits and the beauty of their longboat. "What about three apiece, then?" Still, he sees hesitation. "Come on, lads, for the pride of the ship. If we can get to five pounds, I bet I can get two to one odds from them." Jack looks to Eamon. "Ya haven't spent yer wages yet. Can ya not spare some extra?" Eamon kicks ten shillings into the pot. "And you, Mister Duncan, sir. As first mate, surely ya can wager more than the rest of us." Finally, Jack makes up the difference himself. He leans over the rail and shouts down to the Brits, "Yer honors, I'm sad to say y'are too rich for us. If we scrape together francs, dollars, and pounds, we can only wager five against yer ten. After all, you've got an entire army aboard. Five pounds off our backs is more than ten off yours. It's not that we wouldn't win, because we would, but lucky for you, we can't collect more than five."

There is a pause as the ensign talks to his crew of six. At the end of their muttering, he calls back, "We'll be happy to relieve you of your five pounds then."

"Sir," Jack answers, "to be clear, if yer boat beats ours, you'll take our five, and if our boat beats yers, we will have yer ten?"

"Aye, that will suit us. Are we agreed?"

"Yes, sir, we are." Jack's mates all grin with him.

"Very well. We will return for our winnings after the race."

"Cheeky son of a gun." Jack hushes to his mates.

Atalanta's crew waves and calls their gig over to explain what's at stake. When Mister Strom hears the challenge, he sends Swede back aboard and replaces him with Eamon, who can row harder if the race comes to that. "Be lively now," their mates call as they bear away.

By now, the fleet has tripled. If the wind goes light, the bigger boats will lose. If it picks up, they can stretch out ahead of the rest. It looks like chaos in the midst of the racers. The men at *Atalanta*'s rail shout insults and criticisms and all kinds of advice to the competitors. They laugh at near collisions. The bell rings vigorously aboard the frigate. A white pennant crossed by two broad red lines is hoisted in the rigging.

"Right then, listen up." Mister Strom marshals his crew. "It's a fair wind, but if we fall in with the crowd, they'll block it. So be ready to man your oars and row us to their weather gauge. Once we catch clear air, ship your oars. Toren, you'll be on the mainsheet, and Spanky, you'll trim the jib. Eamon and Coop hike out either side. Keep us on an even keel, and school me on what the locals do."

Excitement builds aboard every boat and among the spectators. Each competitor's focus sharpens. There are shouts from boat to boat, warning off collisions. Still, some boats scrape others. Things are getting frantic. Coop shouts, "Mister Strom! To starboard, behind the jib."

The second mate steers sharply up to the wind, and a bigger boat slips past to leeward. "Well done," he says and steers back down. The gig fast approaches the audience at the end of the pier. "Ready about? Helms a lee." They tack, and Eamon and Coop duck the boom to get to the other side and sit on the gunnel. Sailing back to the end of the starting line, Coop's grin is infectious. Eamon is surprised by his own smile. Half a minute past the boat at the end of the line, they turn to reach back.

The cannon goes off, and too many boats try to fit across the start at the same time. There is a lot of yelling. The ungainly fleet edges away from the start, leaving behind three crew swimming around their capsized boat. "Their fate could have been ours," Spanky admits. Out of self-defense, the smaller boats give way to the larger ones.

The men aboard *Atalanta* can't tell who leads. Their own gig is late for the start while the British longboat is buried somewhere in the middle of the fleet, in too much traffic to put their oars out and row. Three local boats pull away from the confusion. The gig jibes and crosses the starting line to chase them. "Come on, lads!" Jack joins his mates' cheering and pounds a fist on the ship's rail.

"Well done, Mister Strom," Toren reports. "We've got that weather gauge, sir."

"But where are the Brits?"

"I don't see them, sir."

Eamon looks back at the crowd behind them. "Wait. Here they come. They're in the middle, trying to get clear and row."

"Keep an eye on them. The wind's fresh enough that we're sailing faster than we can row."

"Sir," Toren calls, "up ahead, looks like a wind shadow off the shore."

"Right. The leaders will need to bear off and are too big to row. We could catch up to them."

Their attention is pulled back to the long pier when they hear the spectators cheer. The crew of the capsized boat has her upright and are climbing in. The first man in takes the helm and sheets while the other two start bailing. The spectators laugh when the helmsman shakes a fist in the air.

"Good on 'em." Spanky laughs.

To keep wind in their sails, the leaders bear away from the calm. So, they'll sail farther than the rhumb line to get to the first mark. Mister Strom steers for the edge of the calm. "Stand by your oars." As they slow down, it looks like the fleet will overtake them. "Now! Start rowing, and I'll take the mainsheet." The men face aft on their thwarts, slide their oars out, and pull. The boats coming up behind also slow, but the longboat, rowing strong, is coming on. "Put your backs into it. They've got six oars to our four."

"Mister Strom, sir." Spanky gasps between strokes. "The smaller boats . . . behind us . . . they're paddling well inside the calm . . . close to shore. If we're on an ebb . . . a swash channel . . . might be there . . . and favor us. Can you see some chop? Is there current ahead?"

"I can! Good eye. Keep rowing, and I'll get us to that chop. We'll be on the other side of this soon, with wind ahead."

When they get to the wind and ship their oars, the current under them adds to their speed. They are fifth around the anchored boat. They have clear wind for the second leg. The Brits are maybe tenth around the mark, glad to ship their oars and fill their sail. It is a parade to the third mark, some of the bigger boats passing smaller ones. *Atalanta's* gig rounds in eighth place. Eamon and Toren lean out from the high side with each tack upwind. From their perch, they note the Brits are three boats behind and rowing straight for the weather mark. Tacking back and forth through the fleet *and* the anchored boats is an obstacle course. At first, the gig tacks well ahead of their rival, but tacking will cover half again more than the mile to the mark. On the next tack, they cross the other's bow, but finally the Brits cross ahead of them, both boats hurling insults at each other.

"At least we know how to sail!"

"What? Are you too weak to row?"

"Don't worry, men," the second mate encourages his crew, "look at them! They're going against the wind, and they'll tire."

They hear jeers from *Atalanta* as the Brits pass by her and then cheers and advice for themselves. "Well done!" "You can catch 'em." "Keep it up." What catches their attention is a voice from the masthead. "The wind's goin' light outside."

Passing the throng at the end of the pier, calls and cowbells and people banging on pans reenergizes the racers. The frigate's longboat rounds the mark in eighth with *Atalanta*'s gig at ninth. The longboat ships its oars to reach for the mark at the harbor entrance while the gig splits toward the inshore current. When they get to the wind shadow, both boats row. The gig rounds the mark with their opponent close behind. The wind has dropped, and both boats continue rowing. While the Brits are faster, they are heavier. Mister Strom does his best to keep the sails pulling while his crew rows. For the second time, though, they follow the longboat around the mark. There are only five boats ahead of the two of them, all sailing slowly upwind. Cook's choice, the low-slung schooner with the raked masts, is out in front. The leaders are lapping the slowest boats in the fleet. This last leg will be more crowded than the rest. The little boat that recovered from its capsize is in their midst. Her three crewmen grab onto the bigger boat as it passes them to hand-over-hand push themselves alongside and ahead . . . but they are a lap behind.

Studying the boats ahead, Mister Strom finds enough wind close to the beach to ship oars and sail. Meanwhile, the Brits have sailed only one leg of six and are tired. Three oars to a side, knocking back and forth between tholepins, sends the sound of their rowing over calm water. They grin back at the gig and pick a path to keep it astern. The thing about rowing is that the oarsmen face aft. With the ensign at the helm concerned about their rival, no one is looking forward. The men aboard *Atalanta* and in the gig grow quiet when they see the longboat is about to collide with an anchored ship. The men at the front of the longboat sense something. Maybe it's the echo of their efforts bouncing off the hull of the ship they are about to run into. Or they see the shadow of its mast. They shout their alarm, the ensign looks up, steers away, but it's too late. The oars on their starboard side crush against the anchored boat. The ensign is thrown forward onto the men pulling the aft oars, who then fall off their thwart and onto the longboat's sole. The Brits pick themselves up and try to push free as *Atalanta*'s gig sails by in full-throated laughter.

Mister Strom is quick to squelch their howling. "We're not done yet. Keep your focus, watch your trim. Ready about?"

The little gig tacks back and forth close to shore while the bigger boats in the middle of the bay drift toward the finish. Eamon and Coop move to leeward with each tack to help the sails hold what little wind there is.

"The bottom's comin' up," Toren says as they close with the beach.

"Helm's a lee," the second mate responds, and they tack out.

Hearing the sound of oars on tholepins, they all look aft. A hundred yards back, the longboat is coming on but with four oars instead of six.

A clamor arises from *Atalanta*'s decks and rigging. "Row, Mister Strom! You've got to row!" "Go, you sons of guns, go!" Their calls are lost when the chatter on the pier turns into cheers for the schooner crossing the finish. The second mate and his crew give up all finesse. "That's it, lads, we've got to row now!" And they do, for all they are worth. It takes a few strokes before they hit their stride. They glide across the finish line in fourth place and twenty yards ahead of the longboat.

CHAPTER 24

IN A LIGHT breeze, *Atalanta* sails to Port Louis. With only a sweep instead of a rudder, they balance her course up or downwind by trimming, easing, hoisting, and dousing sails at the bow and stern. All the while, the anchor is kept ready. At the end of the day, the exhausted men row the longboats to tow *Atalanta* into harbor.

The next day, alongside the shipyard's quay, the crew starts shipping aboard timber and sailcloth at Chips's and Swede's directions. They have the bowsprit and some sails to replace while the yard fabricates the new rudder, gudgeons, and pintles. The men work between breakfast and supper, after which they have their day's pay and shore leave.

While the rest of the crew works, Eamon and Moses seek out the local merchants. In anticipation of the shipyard's bill, instead of trading goods, they sell them. The islanders soon become enthralled with exotic fabrics, porcelain ware, spices, and fresh tea. At his first audience with the governor, the captain gives Sir Robert a generous selection of fine samples.

"As you can see, your honor, we *are* a merchant vessel. Our cargo is unrelated to your war with France."

"Still, you'll find we are blockading French and American ports."

"Then we shall trade in Britain, sir. Why should we not? Our goods are domestic, not military. Then there is the rest of Europe and South America. If I were not in need of funds, I would be trading here for sugar."

"You *are* sailing between two warring countries, Captain. If we don't claim your ship, our enemy might, and *that* cannot be permitted."

"With respect, sir, there are more than your two countries in this world. The rest of us are not yet yours to divvy up between you. A prize court would not surrender *Atalanta* to either of you. We have not been taken by any ship, so there is no prize to be awarded. We had no choice but to sail into your hands. Should a British ship run afoul of the weather in the Chinese Sea, should she not be able to limp safely into Hong Kong?"

"Certainly, she should."

"And so should *Atalanta* here. Any other course would, in fact, be piracy and holds commerce itself hostage. You captured this island because the French were raiding from here. If you take *Atalanta* now, you'll be raiding Chinese trade and entitling China to take *your* ships."

"Commodore Rowley captured Mauritius for us. His view might differ sharply from yours."

"Shall we have the Commodore repeat Captain Parker's inspection? I would plead my case before him, but does he have your authority to grant *Atalanta* clearance? What I seek is a letter that vouches for our neutrality. Were this still Isle de France, I would seek the same from a French governor." The captain adds, "A letter like that would be of value to me."

On their twelfth day in Port Louis, Captain Rolinson settles *Atalanta*'s bill, and she is towed to anchor in the harbor. Away from being spied upon, he calls for all hands. "Well done, men. It appears we'll not be ready to sail for two or three days, but we leave tonight." Some of the crew nod their approval. "Aye, if we wait any longer, we may never sail again, unless it's in the royal navy. I, for one, will not be recruited, and I cannot live ashore. Not with saltwater in my veins. It so happens the governor is entertaining British officers tonight, and there's no moon. To avoid suspicion, you'll go ashore after supper as usual, but don't tell a soul that we'll be off. Not a whore, not a barkeep, don't even talk of this amongst yourselves. Not a word! And if you're not with us, at the least, don't double-cross your mates." He can only hope. "I want the second watch waiting at the short pier at two bells and the first watch at four. Our ship is ready to fly every sail, her bottom is clean, and she'll be fast. If we see no sail in pursuit, you'll have Cook's best and an extra ration of grog tomorrow." He pauses and looks the men in their eyes. "Right then, dismissed. And remember, say nothing."

Once ashore, unsure if one of their own might betray them, the men keep an eye on each other. They go to their usual haunts in groups of three or four and run up a tab where they can. When Spanky gets back from the arms of a whore, he nods with a wink to Jack.

"Bonsoir, messieurs." One of the shipyard carpenters surprises them at the bar and hoists his mug to theirs. "You'll be off soon, yes?"

"Bonsoir, Andre." Jack hopes he hides alarm from his face. "Yes, we'll be ready in a few days."

"If the Breetish don't take your ship like they took our island." He is a wiry little man, maybe forty years old.

"There is that. Have you heard more rumors?"

"No, but who needs rumors? Of course, they'll take your ship, especially now that she looks good again."

"I hope you're wrong, but what can we do either way? We had no other option."

"What about crew? Are you looking for any?"

"No. Besides, who would sign on when they don't know if she'll still be ours?"

"I might."

Jack squints at the Frenchman.

Andre's smile leaves him, and he lowers his voice. "Jacque, I know ships, so you don't fool me. You're more ready to sail than you appear. It's obvious when you know what to look for. I was explaining it to Stephen, the tall African who works under me."

"And who else were ya explaining this to?" Jack hisses. He scans the patrons nearby. The bartender is at the other end of the bar.

"No one." Andre shrugs. "But I don't know about Stephen. I suggested he say nothing and go pack a bag if he wants to ship out."

"This doesn't bode well." Jack worries. "What about his family or friends?"

"His father drinks too much, and Stephen needs to escape him. My wife died years ago, and I have no children. Look, I can talk to the English if you'll not take us with you, but I don't owe them anything. In fact, I do not like them."

"Where is Stephen?"

"He's outside, across the street."

"Let's go talk to him." They drain their mugs and head for the door, Spanky with them. Jack motions for a few crewmates to follow. They find Stephen in an alley, sitting on his duffle. "I need to know who you've talked to, if this has gotten out."

"I told no one!" the young man protests. "But you'll take us, won't you?"

"I cannot say. I'm not the captain, but ya know that." He looks over his shoulder to see Toren and Vasco catching up and then back to Stephen. "Who saw you carrying a seabag? Damnit! How do I know if we can trust ya? And if we can't trust ya, you're no use to us anyway. We could hog-tie and gag ya right here, keep ya out of the way . . ."

"You can trust us." Andre' meets Jack's glare.

"We'll see about that. Meet us at the long pier at two bells."

"But Jack," Spanky starts to say, and Jack cuts him off.

Once the four mates are back in the pub, Jack asks him, "Were ya gonna say somthin' out there?"

"Aye, but I figured it out. We're meeting at the small pier, and you told them the long pier."

"Right. If they're by themselves, we'll bring 'em."

"What if they're not alone?"

"We might have a fight on our hands."

Captain Rolinson doesn't know how much loyalty to hope for

from his crew. He is nervous waiting aboard *Atalanta* and scowls when Jack shows up with two new recruits. "Curse you," he hisses, "I said not a word!"

"Sir, I didn't say a thing. These two did all the talking."

The old man pauses. "Fair enough. Take 'em below to stow their bags. Then keep 'em on deck. No goin' aloft for them tonight." He's relieved an hour later when the rest of the crew climbs aboard. "Leave the longboats astern until we clear the harbor. Pulling them up now would look suspicious. Clew and bunt lines are ready to let go. The rode is up short. First watch, lay aloft. Moses, take some men to weigh anchor, quietly. Second watch, man the braces, halyards, and sheets. Mates, keep your orders to a whisper. As soon as we're adrift, I want every sail set and faster than ever."

Coop is up and down in the rigging as *Atalanta* spreads her wings. The captain and crew keep looking over their shoulders for any sign of alarm, but so far, everything is quiet. It's a brisk wind. If anyone is watching from shore, the sails silently appear from thin air when they fill with a snap. As they clear the harbor entrance, Coop is atop the mainmast. At his last chance, he waves one arm high overhead. Eamon waves back from the beach, watching *Atalanta* vanish and surprised by his mixed emotions.

CHAPTER 25

SAILORS WITHOUT A berth regard ships with something like lust in their eyes. At first, it's flirtation. They look for signs that a ship is in good repair and her crew proud of her. Is she in need of paint? How well are the sails furled? Is the crew indolent or do they step livelily? Can music be heard coming from her decks at night? When a ship's boat is rowed to shore and tied to a dock, the homeless sailor walks casually by for a better look. The captain and crew have seen it a hundred times and aren't surprised that their suitor chances upon them at a pub. "That's a fine-looking ship you're on. Are you her master or mate? What cargo do you carry? Where are you bound?" It takes courage to ask, "Are you looking for crew? I'm looking for a berth." Even more so after being turned down a few times.

For their part, the master and crew hope they have the luxury of choosing whom they sail with. One bad crewman, someone who shirks his duty or sows discontent, can more than ruin a voyage. Failings have the potential to sink a ship or kill crew. "How long have you been at sea? What ships were you on? Where have you sailed? Did you have any rank?"

At Port Louis, Eamon talks to the yard about ships they might suggest. After the first week with no luck, he returns to Grand Bay. Unwilling to imagine a battle at sea, he refuses to consider the British warships. After a month, he is losing heart. He worries that he may never escape the island. After paying for lodging and replacing what clothes he didn't secret off of *Atalanta*, his money is getting low, and he is at a loss for what work he might find. Maybe he should have stayed with *Atalanta*. His doubts are compounded by a loneliness that surprises him. He hadn't realized he would miss Coop and Jack and a few others. At least he is relieved to be away from Mister Duncan.

One sunny afternoon, he sits on a bench at the end of the long pier, again scanning the bay and critically eyeing the boats at anchor. Most look like they'd be lucky to cross the harbor without sinking. The rest are fishing boats and their captains not known for sobriety.

Half a dozen African men in straw hats and old clothes fish from the pier. Their lines in the water, small buckets of bait near them, they wait for a bite and banter back and forth in a language Eamon doesn't understand. Each man seems to be attended by his own gull, imperiously strutting back and forth nearby, clucking and, once in a while, laughing out loud. There are whiffs of tobacco smoke in the air. The oldest man dozes on the bench. Eamon feels drowsy too.

"Bonzou!" someone says. This is followed by a silence that wakes Eamon. "Kisasayay?" another voice asks. As Eamon rouses, he follows where the men look out to the entrance of the bay. A gaff-rigged topsail schooner, maybe half *Atalanta*'s size, charges in with a bone in her teeth. Full and by in fresh wind, her sails look as if they are cast in bronze; nothing in their trim trembles. She flies the French tricolor snapping at her transom. As the schooner barrels toward the pier, the chatter turns from interest to concern. Collision becomes a real possibility. The fishermen retreat in such a hurry that a few leave their pole and bucket behind. The gulls lurch skyward, screeching their objections. Only Eamon and the old man on the bench are left, Eamon transfixed and the old man waking groggily. Then they are both on their feet and at the pier's railing, looking up at the schooner's rigging and down at her decks. A few feet away, she slides past the end of the pier and turns smartly up into the wind. Her jibs come down immediately. Her helmsman is laughing. The old man shouts down at the schooner, "Bruno!" followed by curses beyond Eamon's ken. As her way carries her into the wind, the schooner's foresail is dropped. When she comes to a stop, so does her anchor. Chain pays out as she drifts aft, and the mainsail is lowered and furled. All this is done by a crew of seven. Eamon studies the schooner's transom to read her name: *Voilà*.

The fishermen scamper back to the end of the pier, shaking their fists but hooting friendly hellos. Hemp fenders are tied in place along the side of the hull. She is close enough to the pier now for a heaving line to arc high through the air from the schooner's stern to the pier. Then another from her bow. The fishermen pull the thin strings; each string pulls a thick mooring line. These have large loops spliced at their ends. The men on the pier drop the loops over the tops of two pilings, and the crew soon settles the schooner alongside, below a loading boom.

This entire maneuver is orchestrated smoothly and precisely. What catches Eamon's attention is that no one was shouting orders. He looks down to the schooner's deck and sees a man with a duffle bag over his shoulder, shaking hands with the helmsman and the rest of the crew. He then climbs up the dock's barnacle-encrusted ladder and hurries off toward town. This apparent camaraderie confuses Eamon. Two sailors adjust the mooring lines while two others remove hatch covers from the main hold.

Eamon sees a dozen men already pulling two large carts out on the pier, the harbormaster at their fore. He is impressed at how fast news on the island travels. At the loading boom, they lower a large net of thick cord from one of the carts into *Voilà*'s hold. Casks are loaded into the net. It takes four or five men to hoist the cargo up and another to swing the boom from above the ship to the pier. There, they lower the net and start loading casks onto the carts. A man from the schooner climbs up onto the pier and begins reviewing with the harbormaster a list of cargo to offload.

If *Voilà* is westbound, Eamon determines to do whatever it takes to sail aboard her. He isn't going to let her get away without him, even if he must sleep on the dock, and he looks for how or where he might stow away. *How can I convince them to take me on?* After watching and waiting, Eamon steps in line behind the last man hauling the cargo net up. Timing his effort with theirs feels like hoisting sail on *Atalanta*. The longshoremen loading the carts stop to stare at him. After they lower the net to the dock, the others do the same. In some alarm, the harbormaster shouts at him, louder as he goes on, but Eamon can only motion ignorance.

"He's asking who the hell you are," the schooner man translates. Eamon feels at a loss to answer. "You *are* the only fair-skinned man here besides me."

"I suppose I stand out, eh?" Eamon tries to smile at the man's tired amusement.

"Yes, you do. So, who are you?"

"Eamon McGrath, sir, able seaman, and I'm without a ship, looking for a berth. Are you *Voilà*'s master? Is it Bruno?"

Bruno puts up a hand to interrupt. "Let's talk about this after we finish unloading." He says something to the harbormaster who then shrugs. "If you want to work for free . . ." Bruno breaks off mid-sentence. "Merde!"

Looking over his shoulder to see what stopped the conversation, Eamon sees Captain Parker with four marines coming toward them. Bruno says a few words to the harbormaster, and the men carry on unloading. He then strides to meet the Englishmen and salutes them. "Congratulations on your capture of Isle de France."

"Thank you. Captain Parker, at your service. Note that we have reverted the island to her former name of Mauritius. From where are you arriving?"

"We're here from India, sir."

"And what is your cargo?"

"Mostly salt, sir. And tea."

"Very well. While my sergeant steps aboard to inspect your ship, I'll want to see your log and manifest. You'll open these two casks, as well." He points. "If we find contraband, we will confiscate your ship."

"Of course, I understand." Bruno holds himself in check. "I'm sure you'll find no problem." Captain Parker's attention stops on Eamon among the longshoremen and Bruno adds, "He's new crew."

"Very good."

After an hour, the Brits seem disappointed to find nothing amiss and leave.

"You'll take me on then?" Eamon doesn't wait to ask.

"That was to fend the arrogant bastards off. Put your back into it and we'll see."

By the time they finish unloading, it is dusk, and Eamon is bone-tired. Bruno takes pity on him. "You've worked harder than you had to. We can at least feed you, but don't mistake that as taking you on. Just come below and have a meal."

Eamon follows Bruno down to the deck and aft of the mainmast. There, they descend the companionway ladder to *Voilà*'s quarters. The dark wood interior, burnished by time and wear, glows beyond the warmth of the lamplight. Under and over the aromas from the galley, the smell of the ship feels intimate and familiar to Eamon. A line creaking somewhere in the rigging completes the ship's embrace.

Aft of the companionway ladder is a long table surrounded on three sides by bench seats. Above the seat backs are berths, two to a side, head to foot, and one aft athwartship, each with its own privacy curtain tucked open for the moment. The seat backs extend above the inboard edge of each berth such that someone sleeping can't fall out regardless of what tack *Voilà* is on or how far she heels. Forward of the ladder is the galley and larder, the bulkhead between them bisected by the base of the mainmast. To either side of the galley, a short corridor leads forward. A door outboard of each indicates a cabin to port and another to starboard. Another bulkhead forward closes off the end of the corridors and the crew's quarters from the ship's main hold, which fills the hull between the two masts. Eamon remembers looking down from the pier and seeing the hatch to another hold forward of the foremast.

Two men sit at the table. A third pours a draft of beer at each of six places while a fourth cooks. Eamon is relieved to hear them chat in English. "Did you see them run?"

"That *was* fun, wasn't it? I've never seen that lot move so fast."

Looking at the cook, Bruno chimes in, "You *did* cut that a bit close."

"Lord help us if one of them had a fish on and we clipped his line," says the portly old man in the galley with an Irish brogue.

"He wouldn't have let go!" someone adds. "We'd have pulled him into the water."

Bruno goes to the galley and picks out another place setting before going to sit at the table. "Mates, we have a guest tonight. He fancies himself a sailor, though he looked more like a longshoreman today. He's looking for a ship. Bid welcome to . . ." He doesn't remember Eamon's name.

"Eamon, sir. Eamon McGrath."

"And watch out. He works for free," Bruno jokes.

The cook looks over his shoulder. "Now *there's* a proper Gaelic name."

Each man takes turns shaking Eamon's hand. Half a head taller than all of them, Marco looks immensely strong yet is so soft-spoken that Eamon isn't sure of his name. The youngest member of the crew, at maybe twenty-five, his skin tone bespeaks Mediterranean ancestry. He is pouring the beer. Harper, a wiry little middle-aged African with deep crow's-feet at the corners of his eyes, pulls a pipe from his mouth to say *bonsoir*. His base voice has a local accent. He is carving something onto a whale's tooth. Smith is of mixed race, about Eamon's size and age. He drops a big tomcat from his lap as he stands up. "Dat's Mouser." His gaze is direct and wary. From the galley, Eamon hears, "Call me Cook, of course. Welcome aboard, and let's eat." He then shouts to a forward cabin, "Admiral!"

The last crewmember arrives from the port cabin, pats Cook on the shoulder, and reaches for Eamon's hand. "You can call me Admiral, but my name is Sophie." Eamon is caught off guard. Looking down from the pier, he had seen her working, but she dresses as a man. She is tall, with an athletic ease. Her black hair is cropped short, and her chest is flat. "Bruno's my husband, and Cook is my papa." This doesn't relieve Eamon's shock, so she gives up trying. "Are you hungry?"

"I apologize," he stammers, "I've never seen a woman wear trousers, unless it was in Hong Kong."

"Not sure we'd recognize her in anythin' else," Cook adds. They all follow his lead through the galley and come back to the table with full bowls of chowder. Marco carves fresh bread into big chunks and passes it around.

"Have you noticed"—Harper winks at Cook—"that we're back now? Maybe you could find something besides seafood at the market."

"Nothin' will be as fresh as the fish you catch." Cook raises his stein in reply. "Don't worry, though. We'll have beef tomorrow night and fresh vegetables with it."

Small wonder that sitting down to a meal together is sacred to every culture. Is there a more ancient way to meet and be met?

Marco and Harper fished with their fathers as youngsters. Marco in Spain and Harper from Isle de France. Smith escaped slavery in America and bears only his former master's surname. His skin a lighter shade of brown. His master sired him . . . to say "fathered" would be a crime against the word. Long ago, Bruno was in the French navy. When he arrived at Isle de France, he resigned his commission to buy and refit *Voilà*. She'd been a mess, but he recognized speed in her lines. Out of a hunger for adventure, he has expanded his trade routes. Cook served in the English navy before any of them were born. He was working aboard *Voilà* when Bruno bought her. They sailed together for a few years before Cook's wife died in Dublin and young Sophie was shuffled off to relatives Cook knew nothing of. He convinced Bruno that Ireland is a small detour from a trip to Europe. Maybe they could find a better home for his daughter or Cook could find a new wife. It appears easy to convince Bruno to sail to any place new to him. By the time they arrived, Sophie was seventeen, and her

living was bitter and hard. Once Cook found her, she was damn near
wild, and he wouldn't leave without her. They decided to bring her
back to Isle de France. En route, she proved to be not a passenger
but a strong hand. She continued as crew, and after a few years, she
and Bruno married.

Their stories—in fact, this entire experience—are outlandish to
Eamon. Aboard *Atalanta*, there had been a strict hierarchy and harsh
boundaries. Here, he and the crew and captain all dine together,
almost like a family, which three of them are. *These people seem*, dare
he think it, *happy*. This is a radical thought that he is unable to trust.

It turns out that the man who departed *Voilà* earlier in the day is
a local. They had returned in time for him to join his pregnant wife,
and he signed off of *Voilà*. Eamon's hopes buoy. When he learns that
Voilà is westbound, it's too much. He casts his eyes down to the table.
"Gentlemen . . . and lady, I've told you my story and listened to yours."
He looks up to plead his case. "If you sign me on, you'll not regret it.
I can work as hard as anyone. My last ship literally whipped me into
shape. I've been 'round the Horn and over the line. I've weathered
a cyclone and a shipwreck. And I was almost an apprentice to my
captain. Except for using a sextant, I can navigate. I'll do anything it
takes to return to my family. You can take advantage of that. You jest,
but yes, I'll work for free if I must, and when you turn your course
east, I'll look for another ship, but please try to understand that I
have *got* to sail with you. As far west as you'll go." In the silence that
follows, he wonders if they are embarrassed for him.

"Easy Eamon," Sophie answers. "We're for you for certain, but
we haven't sailed with you before."

"We're a small ship and small crew," Bruno adds. "We can't afford
to take the wrong man with us." He pauses. "Why don't you join us
for Saturday's race?" The rest of them nod approval. "If we like how
you sail, we'll consider signing you on."

❋ ❋ ❋

Eamon shows up two days later with his duffle packed. "Just in case," he explains. He is worried to see twice as many men aboard, but it turns out it takes more crew to race around the buoys than to cross an ocean. Still, they all look able, and no doubt a few are vying for the empty berth.

Voilà is in luck. She needs a windy day to race, and she's got one. Eamon is glad he's been in the race before, albeit in a tiny boat. He hopes to impress Bruno and the rest by anticipating what will be called for. Without the added wagering, only ten or twelve local boats show up. The start is a much more orderly affair than Eamon remembers. At the first mark, he stands ready to haul in the mainsheet before gybing. Tacking up the third leg, he and Harper are in charge of the jib sheets. Eamon is given the helm for the fourth leg and drives *Voilà* around the mark in sync with the crew's sail handling. On the last leg, he calls out the traffic they dodge, glad that he isn't steering anymore. Back at anchor near the pier, Eamon helps furl sails. He coils lines while the rest of the crew chats on the back deck at a keg of beer. When he joins them, they toast their near victory; the boat with the raked masts was the winner again. *Voilà* came in second.

"You haven't sailed on a schooner before, have you?"

Eamon turns to Harper. "Was it that obvious?"

"You avoided the topsails."

"Never sailed with one that wasn't square-rigged. Wasn't sure what to do with them."

"Don't worry," Cook says. "You stuck to what you know."

When Sophie meets his eyes, she raises a toast. "To our new crewman." He nearly cries with relief.

"Be ready to load cargo tomorrow," Bruno adds, "and sail the day after. Welcome aboard."

"Thank you. It can't be too soon." Eamon drinks deep, feeling his fate could be turning at last. When night falls, he finds himself sitting on the cabin top, another beer in hand, and listening to Marco play guitar. Looking to the western horizon feels new to him. For the first time, he can almost picture home there beyond it. Life ashore is sweetest to a sailor before sailing, the breeze never so fragrant. Eamon, though, is more than ready to leave Mauritius astern. He sleeps aboard that night and the next. He isn't about to risk any chance of *Voilà* sailing without him.

CHAPTER 26

COOK STEERS WHILE everyone else hoists sail. Marco proves to be twice as strong as anyone else. Once clear of Mauritius, *Voilà* meets twenty knots of wind. As she comes alive, so does her crew. They are coiling lines and squaring away the deck when Cook sings out a song. With uncertain voice, Eamon picks up its chorus by the time it ends. He glimpses his mates smiling to each other as their ship charges ahead. They check with Bruno about getting more speed from her.

"Do you want a topsail?" Sophie asks.

"Not yet. Let's settle in for a bit. Eamon and I will take the first watch. You and Smith the second. That leaves Marco and Harper for the third."

"Three watches, sir?" Eamon asks.

"Yes, three hours each. That gives us six hours off, but at night, the last half is on standby. Chores, of course, during daylight. Cook doesn't stand watch, but he's good about steering for sail changes and maneuvers."

"Three hours on and six off sounds luxurious."

"Don't worry. You'll work as hard as you ever have. Now, steer us southwest while I make a log entry. We'll raise an island in a day and leave it to starboard. That will be Réunion."

In short order, the differences between life aboard *Atalanta* and *Voilà* become obvious and are profound. After more than a year of never being able to relax, out of habit, Eamon feels tense. His new mates make sport of him when he stumbles over Sophie's orders with, "Yes, sir. Or ma'am, I mean. Pardon me."

"'Admiral' will do." They laugh.

"You're tryin' too hard, man."

"Aye, stop sayin' 'sir' so much."

"I don't know, lads." Sophie smiles. "I don't mind 'sir', and Bruno is startin' to like the sound of it."

A week after Réunion, they pass south of Madagascar. The rhythm of voyaging feels familiar to Eamon. He's surprised to think it may even be comforting. Day and night, keeping *Voilà* moving is a ritual of faith. Faith that their destination is real, and their days will bring them to it. After all, it has a name, and doesn't a name mean it cannot be a fiction? By arriving, their faith is rewarded.

Most mornings, Cook comes up on deck to admire the sunrise. He brings hot mugs of coffee or tea for whoever is on deck and one for himself. He checks for eggs in a knee-high row of cages that suffice as a chicken coop and then goes below to cook breakfast. If they're lucky, it'll be eggs layered with cheese and, while the produce lasts, vegetables. More often, it's porridge and biscuits. Still, Eamon remarks that he hasn't eaten this well in a long time, and Cook shrugs. "Bruno is French. He thinks he is a gourmet and wants good food."

The chiming of the ship's clock stamps an abstract upon everyone's days. Otherwise, 'time' is as fluid as the water they sail through. At night, it is often Cook who shakes them awake. "Yer on deck at the next bell. Kettle's on the stove." He goes back to the starboard cabin as they climb out of their berths.

Eamon comes up on deck yawning and rubbing his eyes. He orients to the wind and waves and admires the moonlight dappling the water's surface. "Nice night."

"Wind's dropped some." A whiff of pipe smoke confirms it's Harper at the helm. "We changed to the yankee on the headstay."

"That's a big sail. I'd have helped with that."

Sometimes they wait for the next watch to change sails together. But each watch takes pride in letting the others sleep by taking care of changes on their own and never arriving late for their turn on deck. Their pride spills into competition. Who left the decks more organized? Which team sailed *Voilà* faster?

"Don't worry," Harper answers. "Cook steered for us, and Bruno was up early. He's making a log entry now."

"He doesn't sleep much," Eamon observes.

"The good captains don't. He works as hard as all of us put together."

The size of the silhouette coming aft belongs to Marco. "Jib's furled on the bowsprit," he reports.

"What's our course?" Eamon asks.

"Due west." Harper pulls a puff on his pipe, trying to illuminate the compass with its glow. "Are you ready?"

"Aye." Eamon takes the wheel.

Harper stands by until he sees Eamon settle the course. He sighs. "She's yours," he says as he goes below.

"Sweet dreams," Eamon answers.

❋ ❋ ❋

Unlike Captain Rolinson, Bruno keeps his crew informed of where they are and where they're going. With a chart spread out on the table and Cook at the helm, he explains to the rest, "We'll close with the African coast in a few more days. There's a Portuguese fort in a big natural harbor." He points. "They always need supplies, and we've done well there before. After that, we can take a day or two off before carrying on. From there, we'll hug the coast for a week to catch a southbound current close in. There's a large shelf south of the continent where there can be bigger waves than we want to see. So, we'll bear away for five days before turning for Cape Town. All told, it could take two or three weeks to get there. We'll sell some cargo, buy ivory and animal skins, and reprovision then."

"How cold will it get?" Eamon remembers rounding Cape Horn and almost shivers.

"It's not so far south, and it will be summer."

Every day, Bruno comes on deck to take the noon sight. Eamon helps by recording the time and measurement. This noon, Bruno offers the sextant to him. "Do you want to try it?"

Eamon hesitates out of respect but is eager to learn. "Really?" He meets Bruno's eyes. "Of course, I'd be honored."

"Then here. Never handle it without the lanyard around your neck. Drop it once, and it's a worthless thing." Eamon does as he's told and grips the obvious handle. "Now then, squeeze this clamp to slide this bar along the arc. Watch how that controls the index mirror . . ."

In Maputo, Marco accompanies Bruno to sell sugar, salt, fabrics, and tea. Cook and Sophie reprovision. Between Harper, Smith, and Eamon, water casks are topped off, and anchor watch is kept. After that, everyone has two days off before departing. The novelty of days off disorients Eamon. He follows Harper and Smith to taste the local brew but leaves them when they stop at a brothel. It is one thing to accept the attentions of a courtesan and quite another to solicit a whore. Smith returns to the ship soon after Eamon. He never sleeps ashore, and Harper often does. Cook remains aboard while Bruno and Sophie stray away. Marco finds a guide, explores the hillsides, and collects a few souvenirs. On the morning before *Voilà* sets sail, he returns, recounting local sights and stories.

Eamon isn't the only one learning something new. After supper one evening, he finds Marco concentrating on a book with Mouser asleep in his lap. "What are you reading?"

Marco holds his place in the book as he shows the spine to Eamon. It's Shakespeare's *The Tempest*. "It starts with a shipwreck."

"So it does." Eamon raises his eyebrows. "Where did you get it?"

"Cook found it for me. He's helping me learn my letters."

"Really? Can you read Spanish?"

"No, but Cook doesn't know Spanish. So, it's English."

"Shakespeare can be a challenge, though. His writing is ornate."

"It helps when we act it out. Cook takes a character, and I take one. Sometimes Sophie helps. Smith can't read, and Harper doesn't care to."

"I'd be happy to help. Remember, I was a printer. I have a love of books and reading. Is this your first one?"

"No, we started with *Sandford and Merton*. We read it over and over."

"I'll leave you to it, then." Back on deck, Eamon shakes his head. *I was a printer? As if I'll not print again, but it's still what I am.*

That night, Cook shows up beside Eamon at the helm and offers him a hot cup of coffee. "Here, take this while I steer for you." They're alone while Bruno is forward, listening to *Voilà*'s heartbeat.

"Thank you. What's he doing up there?"

"He listens to his ship, touches the rigging, feels how she moves. He's always first to find anything that needs attention. A rip in a sail, a sheet too tight, or cargo that's shifted."

"Kind of you to teach Marco to read."

"We're a lit'rate bunch, we Irish, and glad to share it. I've tried to interest Smith, too. Reading will serve them well. Saints be praised, they serve us well."

CHAPTER 27

ARRIVING IN CAPE Town on a sunny afternoon, *Voilà* is the smallest of a dozen ships anchored in Table Bay. Half of them are British warships, the rest merchants and whalers. Eamon looks for and finds an American flag among them.

"Didn't take you long to spot that." Sophie works beside him as they furl the foresail. "It's a whaler."

"You saw it too?"

"Yes, and then watched you. 'Tis filthy work, whaling, but you'll want to talk to her crew. They might be from your neighborhood and going back."

"I will, but that doesn't mean I'll jump ship. These weeks have been good. And we're still heading north and west, are we not?"

"We are, and you're good crew, but don't concern yourself. We'll shove off with or without you."

A flat-topped mountain a few thousand feet tall and wide dominates the landscape. Cape Town is positioned in the few miles between its slopes and the shore. A smaller ridge with a few peaks borders the town's west edge. In this naturally formed bowl—mountain to the south, ridge to the west, ocean to the north—only a narrow approach from the east is open to attack. An imposing fortress at the water's edge guards this gateway. The one pier in the bay is adjacent to the fort. The village itself is laid out in a European grid of single-story markets, storehouses, barracks, and homes. Dirt streets are wide enough for a horse and cart. A random patchwork of small farms spots the terrain toward the slopes. The scene is semi-arid, sparsely forested, rocky, and largely untilled. Almost tropical, there are palm trees.

Leaving Smith on anchor watch, the rest of the crew rows ashore in the longboat. Cook and Sophie head for the nearest market, Bruno for the harbormaster. Harper and Marco lead the way through a sea of black-skinned people, to a tavern. An early crowd is there. Eamon looks past the men in uniform when someone's laugh draws his attention.

"I didn't realize a laugh could have an accent, but *that* was American." His mates agree, and they follow the laughter to three men playing cards at a round table. Their clothes are patched and sooty, their feet bare. One of them is a heavily tattooed Sandwich Islander. Eamon suspects his own appearance is almost like theirs and hopes his aroma isn't. "Ahoy, gents. Might you be from the American whaler in the harbor?"

"Aye, we are," the oldest of them answers. "You use the term 'gents' loosely, but we'll accept the flattery."

"Will you accept a round of beer?" Eamon supposes that he may as well befriend these men if he might ship with them.

"Of course, and thank you, though you don't have to buy our drinks to join our card game."

"No, thank you. I'm sure the beer will cost me less than the game would. I'm curious about your voyage, though. Where do you hail from?"

"New Bedford, Massachusetts."

"Then we're neighbors! I'm from Marblehead. Eamon McGrath." Marco and Harper pull chairs over to the table, and they all sit down.

"I'm Samson. This is Koa and Ben. We're harpooners."

"This is Harper and Marco. We're from the French schooner arrived today."

"Trim little vessel. Saw you come in."

"Thanks. Yes, she's a good ship. Still, I must ask if you're on your way home, and if so, has your ship an open berth?"

"We'll not be turnin' for home for another year at least. We're far from fully laden."

Excited a moment before, Eamon now feels relief and realizes he is content to stay with his new ship. They all trade sea stories until it's time for another round. That's when the men of *Voilà* get up to leave and both crews wish each other good luck. They're about to close the door as they leave but keep it open for someone coming in who stops suddenly.

"Eamon?" It's Vasco from *Atalanta*.

He's the last person in the world Eamon expects to see. When he realizes who it is, adrenaline charges like a bull through his veins. Anyone close enough to witness feels his fear. In an instant, his eyes grow wide, breath stops, and mouth goes dry. Harper and Marco share a confused glance and, by reflex, take a protective step toward Eamon. His thoughts feel like flashes of lightning. *Is Atalanta here? No! How could I not see her? She cannot be in harbor. Even if she is, Rolinson has no claim on me.*

"Eamon!" Vasco reads his mind. "She's *not* here. Don't worry. She's gone."

With one hand on his chest, Eamon reaches the other to Vasco's shoulder, drops his head, and exhales. He looks up. "Pardon me. You surprised me." He tells his mates, "Relax, he was a shipmate," and turns back to Vasco. "How is it you are here? How are you?"

"I'm well. I jumped ship here a month ago. *Atalanta* heads north, but I want to go west. Go home, like you. And many ships stop here."

"Like me?" Eamon shakes his head. "Did the captain say anything about me?"

"I heard him cuss when he knew you were gone. He is angrier, but he's never happy anyway."

"Heavens, you scared me. How is Coop? And Jack?"

"Jack is good. Coop too. He could be mate someday or even captain."

"Yes, he could. Have you found a ship?"

"When the Spanish whaler came in, she signed me on. The hunt sounds exciting, and the crew gets a share of the profits. I can make more money, and they speak my language. We're bound for Argentina tomorrow."

"Well done. I'm on the French schooner that came in today. She's smaller, so she stops where big ships don't go. She's headed north for now."

Marco and Harper are ready to return to *Voilà*. Eamon shakes Vasco's hand. "It's good to see you. Thanks for your help, Vasco, when I needed it."

"You were not so bad. A little crazy, maybe, but sailors, maybe we need to be crazy. Fair winds, Eamon. I pray you make it home."

"You, too."

At supper that night, *Voilà*'s captain and crew marvel at Eamon's chance meeting. It brings up a surprising number of similar stories. Maybe the world isn't so big after all.

CHAPTER 28

NOW THAT BRUNO knows Eamon's abilities, he switches him to Marco's watch and Sophie to his own. This separates the two fisher-sons, and Marco is quick to recruit Eamon. "Harper thinks he knows how to fish, but he's not Spanish. We need to catch bigger fish than he does." It's another competition, but Cook cuts it short when they catch more than they can eat.

Heading north, *Voilà* meets a favorable current and winds. She raises St. Helena, in the middle of the South Atlantic, in three weeks. After selling staples for a day, they push off and reach Ascension Island in a week. Closer to the equator, warm winds grow hot.

It's late at night under a new moon. Eamon is steering when he is struck on the side of his head. "Ow!" He's on his feet, rubbing his head, and finds a flying fish on deck.

"What?" Marco wakes from where he lay nearby.

"It's a flying fish! Hit me in the head."

"Ha! You're not the first."

"It didn't hurt, really. It was more the surprise of it. I grant I could have expected it. I've been seeing them for a long time, and we've been tossing them off the decks every morning, along with the little squids."

"The ones Mouser doesn't eat, you mean."

"Are they any good to eat?"

"The squids?"

"No, the flying fish."

"They taste fine, but they're more work for less food than the bigger fish we catch. But this is a big one."

"Maybe Cook will fry my attacker for revenge."

The doldrums await *Voilà* near the equator. After weeks of fair wind, her crew feels abandoned by its sudden departure. The schooner floats motionless on a flat sea . . . for a week. If *Voilà*'s sails are hoisted, they hang limp. The sun beats down. A shade cloth is stretched over the aft deck to shelter the helm, but with no way on, there's no need to steer. They can turn the wheel, but *Voilà* won't answer. With it centered and lashed in place, she drifts in a slow circle. If they're going anywhere, it's on the current, not the wind. Their progress is invisible. Or maybe backward.

Sunburnt face turned to the cloudless sky, Eamon dumps another bucket of seawater over himself. It runs through his matted hair and beard and soaks his shirt and breeches. He retreats into the shade where everyone is sprawled on deck. There's nothing to do but wait. No one whistles a tune or sings a song anymore. Dice and cards no longer entertain. Scrimshaw and mending their clothes are the last refuge for passing time. Waiting takes its toll more than the heat. Even conversation evaporates.

"Ration yourselves to two cups of water a day," Bruno orders. "We've used up our cask on deck and are halfway through the one in the galley. Once we get moving, we'll not be far from Cape Verde."

"*If* we get moving." It's Harper. "Remember the *Syrene*? She's been driftin' forever in the doldrums, her sails in tatters and no one aboard. No sign of foul play, and longboats still on deck. Where did her crew go? If we see her . . ."

"Don't believe everything you've heard." Bruno cuts him off. "Mysteries like that, we don't need to hear. Keep a sharp eye out for a cloud, not a ghost ship." Silence returns.

Tensions grow as their water supply dwindles and the wind remains absent. On a small ship, there's little to no room for privacy. Everyone knows when anyone takes a crap and looks the other way. Anyone's mood is obvious to everyone else. When Sophie comes on deck in a huff one morning, Eamon makes the mistake of asking, "Are you cross?"

"I ought not be, but I am," she almost shouts. "I ought to be used to it, but I'm not."

"Used to what?"

"To being married to a man with a mistress. A mistress named *Voilà*. On a voyage, he has eyes for no one but her. I might as well be a hired hand instead of his wife."

"I hardly believe that. He put you into his own watch, didn't he?"

"At my insistence, or I'd not see him at all. The same with days off ashore." She stomps off to the bow to be alone.

A few fish hide in the shade of *Voilà*'s hull, but none are a shark. Like Captain Rolinson, Bruno declares it's time to go for a swim and scrape some growth off the hull. They rig a boarding ladder over the side and lines to hold onto. Diving in, slicing through the surface into cool silence feels like a dream. In an instant, hearing, sight, and smell are eclipsed by the water's sudden, enveloping touch. Free from gravity, muscles stretch through more motion, and the full body sensation is pure bliss. Arcing back up to surface, everyone hoots and smiles with relief.

Only Smith stays on deck. "He can't swim," Cook explains.

"*That* makes no sense." Eamon looks up to *Voilà*'s deck. "A sailor who can't swim? We should teach him."

It takes a rope around Smith's chest—and Marco threatening to throw him in—to get him down the ladder and into the water.

"I had a shipmate named Sam who didn't know how to swim," Eamon tells him. "If we had taught him, he might still be alive. Here, grab this line. Now take a deep breath, hold it in, and try to float on your back."

In the meantime, Sophie beats the others in a race around the ship. "I knew you were a mermaid!" Bruno laughs.

That night, a swell starts rolling the ship. They furl the sails to stop them beating back and forth. The incessant motion doesn't have the rhythm of sailing. Even sleep is a challenge. Too hot and muggy below, they string hammocks on deck. Fully laden, *Voilà*'s cargo counterbalances the weight of her masts and dampens the side-to-side rocking. Still, in the morning, they set to tightening what rigging has worked loose. At least the swell foretells wind somewhere.

In the late afternoon, Eamon asks the others, "Am I seeing a mirage or a cloud?"

They all follow his stare to some indistinct gauze on the horizon. Cook's voice comes alive. "If it's a mirage, we're *all* fooling ourselves."

Bruno is eager too. "That should have some wind in it. Hoist sail."

The main, foresail, and flying jib are up when Sophie calls from the ratlines, "What's that? On the swell." She looks again. "A hundred yards out, off the starboard bow." The rest of them follow where she points. "There's another," she calls down, "and two beyond."

Smith climbs up to the fore crosstrees and pauses. "Dey're bodies." He almost chokes. "Black bodies. Slaver my mama was on did dis. She tol' me. Dey got rid of da dead to save da 'cargo' dat's still alive. If dey want to hide what dey done, dey leave da chains on, and da bodies sink. But chains cos' money."

In the space of twenty minutes, *Voilà*'s captain and crew have sprung from sloth to action and now stand still, revulsed. No one notices a wisp of wind until *Voilà* begins to coast forward. Her motion, in turn, breaks their paralysis. She takes them close by the nearest corpse. It's naked and face down.

"Where are the sharks?" Harper wonders aloud.

Marco stares at the dead man they pass and mutters, "Madre de Dios. He looks like he could start swimming. They haven't been in the water long."

"The sharks will be here soon enough," Cook answers, "and birds, if they scavenge this far out."

"That slaver can't be far off." Bruno scans the horizon. "They must've been becalmed like us. Let's get the hell out of here."

By the time they're moving well, they've passed almost thirty corpses. Male, female, and child. Night drops like a curtain behind them, covering what they've witnessed. No one has an appetite for supper.

CHAPTER 29

EAMON AND MARCO are below when they hear distant thunder. They put Shakespeare down and go up on deck. Squalls dot the eastern horizon north and south and march toward *Voilà*. Fair warning of their advance, rumbles echo over smooth water.

Cook is at the helm and grins. "The spawn of Africa," he calls them. He's got *Voilà* on a collision course with the nearest one and it looks mean.

"Time to shorten sail," Sophie confirms. "Bring up our oilskins and get yours on."

To gird for battle, they lower the flying jib and lash it to the bowsprit. They furl the topsails, reef the main, and drop the foresail. After that, they check the lashings on the hatches and the boats overturned on deck. They walk the decks and climb the rigging to check even small details that catch their eye.

There's a barrel lashed to the base of the mainmast and a hose that goes below to its twin in the galley. Bruno is busy attaching a funnel made of sailcloth at the main's gooseneck and beckons to Eamon, "The rain coming off the mainsail will catch along the reefed cloth on the boom and pour toward the mast here. After the water stops tasting salty, lash the funnel to the ring at the top of this hose. We've got the lid off the galley cask and a cheesecloth over it to filter what we catch. When Harper calls it's full, aim the funnel into this cask. Lash it like so. A storm or two will top us off."

Bruno finishes demonstrating and returns to the quarterdeck. The wind picks up and whistles around the rigging, rising in pitch and volume. The air around them dims, and rain bursts over *Voilà*. She heels over and charges up to hull speed. Everyone on deck faces away from the wind-driven rain. After a few minutes, Cook steers *Voilà* off the wind to ride inside the mayhem. After almost an hour, the squall leaves them in its wake, lightning flashing, thunder echoing, pretending victory. Dusk is falling.

"That was a good one," Cook proclaims. "The galley cask is near full. We can try to dodge the rest of them for now. They'll be comin' onto us like clockwork for days."

"After we dry off and have some supper," Bruno calls, "we'll hoist full sail."

It's dark when they go to pull up the main, but when four of them haul away, the belly of the mainsail tears. They all curse and look to Eamon.

"Merde!" Bruno shouts from the helm.

Frightened, Eamon looks from one to the other of his mates and admits, "I . . . I must've left an earring tied. In the dark, I missed it."

It's Cook who conciliates. "Be glad you're aboard *Voilà*. You'd get ten lashes for that on *Atalanta*. Lucky for you, the only cat here is Mouser."

"There's no cat-o'nine-tails?"

"What do you take us for? Savages?" Cook looks insulted.

"What about discipline?"

"Do you see a need for discipline? Brute-force can't accomplish half of what respect can. If we can't respect a man, how can we trust him? And how could he trust us after whipping him? We're too small a crew for it to come to that. We need each other too much."

Bruno calms down and orders, "Lower it down and tuck the reef back in. I'll get the repair kit at daybreak."

❊ ❊ ❊

Days later, Sophie brings coffee up to the dawn watch. Marco is at the helm. Eamon sits on the hatch to the forward hold, watching *Voilà* dance with wind and waves.

"Where did you place your bet for when we'll raise the islands?" she asks Eamon.

"I'm hoping they'll come up here on my watch, but I put my money on noon. What about you?"

"I bet on last night, but I'm always too eager to see it. Remember, half the pot goes to the closest guess, but the other half goes to the one who calls 'Land ho!'"

"Is that why you're up?"

"That, and I find it hard to sleep when we're close. 'Tis magic when a landfall materializes. As if it hasn't always been there. Like it was just now molded and lifted from the sea. Time offers it up, and by some holy rite, we find it. 'Tis a miracle every time." She looks down at her lap and back up.

"You sound like a young sailor I know. Your words for it aren't mine, nor were his, but I feel it, too. You'd think I could describe it, being a printer and words being my life."

"Here's to landfalls." She hoists her own mug.

"To landfalls," Eamon toasts. "What did Bruno guess?"

"He thinks the sunrise will bring the islands up. Could be any minute."

"I'm not sure it's fair he gets to bet. After all, he's the navigator."

"What about you? He says your sights are as good as his."

"I'm flattered."

"Don't be. Bruno doesn't flatter. Flattering would be telling *you*, but he didn't. If he told me, he meant it."

"I'm not betting to win so much. I just want to get back to solid ground and the real world. A step closer to home."

"Not me," Sophie differs. "I'd as soon rebound off the shores and stay at sea. All those people, thank the heavens they don't live out here. *Voilà* is our little world, and 'tis better than the one on shore."

"Sophie, what happened to you there?"

"After mum died, your 'real world' nearly killed me. No one wanted me except for my labor, and I dared not eat more than I could harvest. Like those slaves Smith called 'cargo,' I was 'cargo.' I don't have his scars or yours. Not on the outside, but it hurts a child to know she's unwanted. To be afraid all the time, to trust no one, at everyone's mercy when there's none of it, when the only thing is greed. She can't help but take it personally. Out here, though, nature's indifference is perfect. Pure. Nothing personal about it. There's no wanted or unwanted and no mercy, either. A storm is only a storm. If it kills you, it wasn't trying to. It happens, and you are there when it happens. That's all. There's naught to forgive. People, though, by definition, are personal. We should care, but your 'real world' doesn't care." She finishes her coffee. "If you think about it, that world isn't so real. 'Tis a myth, a house of cards that will be long gone when this"—she sweeps the horizon with a gesture—"will still be here. Waves appear defeated when they retreat from shore, but look at the shards awash below every cliff. I don't know anything more real than the ocean."

"Nor I. I only wish what happened to you hadn't."

"Thanks, but it happened to Smith, too. He rarely goes ashore, and he comes back as soon he can. And you. It wasn't nature that stole you from your life."

Eamon frowns. "Maybe human nature is an element not unlike the rest. Was it Captain Rolinson that took me? He was complicit, a pawn in a human drama, but did he intend to do me harm? I don't think so."

"Do you forgive him?"

"No!" His answer is quick and bitter. "Hell no. I would see him behind bars two years for every year I've been gone. But did *he* do it? Or was he only being human, and 'tis human nature that should be on trial?"

"Good luck with that." Sophie shrugs. "Human nature has long proven itself more curse than blessing."

The bright eastern sky births a blinding crest of sun. *Voilà* heels in a gust, and water sprays from her bow as she rises over another wave.

"Will you tell me about your Rebecca?"

"Oh my! I hope she's still mine. I'm still hers, anyway. Where do I start?"

"Try the beginning. How did you meet?"

Their conversation goes beyond Marco's turn at the helm until he calls, "Land ho!" and laughs. "Half the winnings could have gone to either of you if you looked up. You were talkin' too much."

CHAPTER 30

ONE HUNDRED AND sixty miles in diameter, nine major islands make up the Cape Verde archipelago. Located three hundred and fifty miles west of the African continent and sixteen degrees north of the equator, their weather is hot. From a distance, they appear mountainous and brown. Closer up, heat waves shimmer above their beaches. Colonized by the Portuguese, they are ideally positioned as a stopover along the major shipping lanes. *Voilà* sails between the smaller islands to sell essentials. A lot of other ships come and go, most of them slavers. Anchoring in Mindelo harbor, they top off *Voilà*'s water and provisions.

Marco clears the dishes after the evening meal. Bruno spreads a chart out on the table. Mouser promptly jumps up and onto it. "It's hard to feel it here, but it will be winter soon in the North Atlantic," he tells his crew. "We could wait for the winds to favor us from here to the Canaries and Azores, and then on to Europe. I would aim for the Mediterranean and Italy, but the trade winds will get us to the West Indies in two to three weeks. In the spring, we can think about sailing north and then east. Tomorrow, we'll weigh anchor and head west."

"I'll drink to that," Cook toasts, "a warm winter in the Indies."

"And closer to home," Eamon adds.

They all nod approval and drink to Bruno's plan.

He adjourns with assigning the watches: himself and Sophie; Marco and Harper; Smith and Eamon.

Everyone is on deck that evening, all their senses drinking in the nearby island. They can hear a gentle sea lapping against the beach. Voices carry surprisingly far over calm water. A man's voice. A woman's laugh. A baby's cry more distant. A dog's bark. By the light of the moon, they can't distinguish details, but they can see silhouettes on shore. They smell fires and food and verdure. No matter how salty their blood may run, their biology tells them they belong on land. They may be oblivious to this message, but their bodies cannot ignore it. They linger on deck late into the night while they can almost taste the island. On the foredeck, Marco plays guitar. Cook and Sophie sing a sweet duet. They ask Smith to sing for them.

"Which one?" he asks. "I got songs fo' everyting. Songs fo' workin', songs fo' dyin' and bein' born, and everyting in between. Gettin' married. Happy and sad, mos'ly sad. And songs fo' freedom." When they bid him to choose, his solo base starts. "So tarred! Can't wait for dat sun to go down, so tarred, gonna lay me down to . . ."

It's a week later, the middle watch of another night underway. There's something about traveling at night. Vision can't linger on detail, and inner senses open a bit more; voices seem disembodied. The darkness listens and draws us on to say more. Conversation sometimes strays where it might not in daylight.

Cradled in this, Eamon wonders aloud, "You and I, Smith, we've got scars on our backs, but what else do we have in common?"

"We got families," Smith answers.

"Really? But you never mention yours."

"You got no idea. Do ya?"

"What do you mean? About family?"

"Eamon, you was torn from yo' family. But me, I tore myself from dem. I was da one who cut dem from ma own chest! Can you imagine dat? I knew I'd die if I stayed, but I didn't know I'd half die if I lef'." Eamon doesn't know what to say, so Smith goes on, "Since da day you was gone, you been hopin', tryin' to go back. Haven'tchya?"

"Of course."

"Do you know how I hear dat? Fust, you got hope. Slaves are not born wit' hope. Don't know hope. It's not in d'ey language."

"Without hope, how did you escape?"

"It warn't hope. It were chance. Luck. I'm not sayin' whetha was good luck or bad. My massa"—Smith pauses—"da man who t'ought he own me took me an' anotha slave to Charleston to unload his cotton on da docks. I neva been dare befo' an' bein' dare's too much for me. My eyes almos' fell out my head when I saw nigra sailors. All a sudden, I had to go." His voice starts to crack. "I had to go an' I knew I might neva get anotha chance. It hit me like a bullet. My wife an' I got two chill'n, an' my mama was back dare on da plantation. I knew I couldn't go back to bring 'em. An' if I went back, I couldn't say goodbye. I couldn't leave 'em, an' if I din't leave, I'd die for sho'. You seen da scahs on my back. I got one dem nigra sailors to hide me, an' I went."

In the silence that follows, Eamon shakes his head. "I felt like a slave on *Atalanta*."

"Ain't da same tin'." Smith's voice is quiet. "Not da same a'tall. After da islands, we probly go to America, but I won't leave dis ship. Most da whole time, I be scared of bein' seen. I paid too high a price for freedom to lose it. Leavin' was too hard. I couldn't do it again. Before I let anyone take me back, I'll t'row mysef into da sea. Like dey did at Igbo."

"But you can swim now."

"Don't know 'bout dat, but I swear I wouldn't try."

The night air feels colder than before. The rumble of *Voilà*'s bow wave and the hiss of her wake is the only conversation left until Eamon breaks the silence. "What if I can draft freeman's papers for you? When I get back to my press, I could copy someone else's papers. I'm sure I could make them look real. Official enough that you could be free."

"I *am* free . . . 'ceptin' for my ghosts, and no paper go'ne chase dem away."

"Listen to yourself, though. You'll be hiding. Nervous. What if . . ."

"No, suh!" Smith's voice booms full of emotion. "I took my

freedom wit' no paper an' don't need none to keep it. Da sooner we leave America da better. Dis ship is my home. I been safe here. Dese folks are da closest t'ing I got to family, an' it's close enough. I don't want no one too close."

"Pardon me, Smith. I was tryin' to help."

"Pardon me, too. I din't mean to get mad atchya."

❋ ❋ ❋

Grenada is *Voilà*'s first stop in the Caribbean. From there, they island-hop north, up the West Indies, and indulge in this thing called a "day off" as they go. They're not in a hurry. In fact, they are stalling, hoping for a short winter. Of course, Eamon is eager to carry on. He would look for another ship but realizes none of them are better than *Voilà*.

The British have taken over several islands. So, Bruno is discrete. *Voilà* sails at night more than in daylight and anchors in bays removed from the main ports. When they get to Puerto Rico and Cuba, Marco celebrates his native tongue. In their travels, they learn Mexico's war for independence is full-blown, and the United States is at war with England.

It is December 1812.

"With America embargoed, goods are scarce, and our profits should be handsome." Bruno tells his crew. "It will take some luck to slip past a blockade, but we are more weatherly than their big ships. As long as we stay beyond the range of their guns, we can outpoint them to the weather gauge. It would take us out of our way, but we should be able to elude them. We can likely sneak past once or twice, but I don't want to make a habit of running blockades."

"Don't let him fool you," Sophie cuts in. "We all want to see how Eamon fares when he gets home."

Bruno shrugs and grins. "Maybe we do, but it's not as if we weren't goin' anyway, so we may as well aim for Marblehead. They'll not expect us near winter that far north, and the blockade could be more porous in bad weather."

"So much for a warm winter," Cook complains.

"Don't worry," Bruno answers. "We'll have more time between the islands before we turn north. Soak up the sun while you can."

Upon hearing "Marblehead," Eamon is in a daze until Smith brings him back to the moment. "Eamon, I been tinkin' 'bout dem papers."

"What?"

"Freeman's papers. You said you could make me some when you get home. I was tinkin' it couldn't hurt to have 'em."

Eamon shakes his head to gather himself. "Of course. Anything I can do, but there's one thing you'll need."

"What's dat?"

"A first name."

When they explain their conversation to the others, they all start offering names.

"How about George? Like George Washington."

"You've got to keep it simple, something that won't attract attention."

"But you don't look like a George. What about John or Thomas?"

The suggestions won't stop until Smith has his counterfeit papers in hand.

"Like we're namin' a newborn babe," Cook declares.

CHAPTER 31

IT'S MARCH BY the time *Voilà* rides north on the Gulf Stream and a south wind. Eamon wears every piece of clothing he has against the cold. Cook keeps a hot kettle on the stove all day and night for the crew to warm themselves.

They sail close enough to the coast to spy two Royal Navy ships patrolling the entrance to Charleston. "Let's keep our distance from that," Bruno calls. "Get ready to jibe," and they tack away, out to sea. A day later, the wind shifts to westerly, and he's doubly glad to be beyond the Gulf Stream. "In the northern hemisphere, winds shift in a clockwise direction," he explains. "Like looking down at a clockface printed on the chart, with north at twelve o'clock. If it shifts from south to east, or six to three, it's called 'backing' because it would be backwards for a clock, and the wind will come *back* to south. If it shifts from south to west, it usually goes on 'round to north, and it's called 'clocking.' We'll be glad we aren't in the Gulf Stream with a north wind. Many a ship has foundered there when that happens, especially off Cape Hatteras, where the shore reaches out."

"Can we not weather that?" Eamon almost complains. "Otherwise, we're sailing away from where we want to go. To go a thousand miles, we're sailin' two."

"We don't *want* to weather that."

"Y'know, Eamon," Cook interjects, "you could do well to apply this to the rest of your life." Eamon rolls his eyes and Cook goes on, "I know you're eager to get home, but how can I explain it? Let's say there's something you want. I don't know, maybe it's a hug or a kiss.

Or a new pipe. You tell your wife, 'This is what I want,' and she says no. She's like the wind. You can't come straight at her. So, do you give up? Or do you start tacking and eventually get what you want."

"Forgive me if I'm closer to home than I've been in more than two years, closer than I dared hope, but we were maybe a week, ten days away. When will we tack back?"

"We'll tack back after this cold front passes and the wind shifts." Bruno pauses. "But not if it goes west."

Eamon realizes he's supposed to fill in an answer. "Because it will go back to the north. We'll tack when it shifts to the east."

"Right. That settled. I'll rely on you to watch the wind. I'm gonna lay down before my watch."

Two days later, they beat against the north wind. After four more days, their tack is toward the coast when they're swallowed by a dense fog. A day more of sailing blind, it's dusk when Bruno and Eamon study the charts at the big table below. They pour over dead-reckoning notes, trying to guess where they are.

"Our last good fix was before the fog, there." Eamon points to the chart. "And here's our time and distance."

"But at three or more, the Gulf Stream has swept us well north."

"How long have we been in it?"

"A few days by now."

"So, it's pushed us maybe a hundred miles north. You've offset that with a west-northwest course. That should put us in . . ." Eamon walks off the distance and direction with dividers.

"To Boston," Bruno finishes, "which we should give a wide berth. British ships will be patrolling there."

"Why not come into the north, then?"

"Only if this fog lifts. It's a rocky coast. Islands and reefs project from shore and rise in a hurry. The lead line can't give enough warning, and I don't trust the charts I have for there."

Harper appears at the companionway and interrupts, "Cap'n, I hear a ship's bell."

Bruno meets Eamon's eyes. If there's a ship nearby and they're chiming the hours, it may be a navy ship. On deck, the rest of the crew is studying the fog in every direction. The wind is light, and *Voilà* almost drifts at a few knots.

Bruno whispers to them, "Can you point to where it came from?" They all point in different directions. "Merde!" He looks up to guess the depth of the fog and sees no blue sky. "Harper, lay aloft. Let me know if the fog thins up there, and watch for their masts. If you call down, try to whisper. Cook's on the helm, Marco and Eamon on the headsails, Sophie on the fore. I'm on the main. Be ready to tack."

They can hear voices but not yet words. Whoever it is, they're getting closer. Time stands still. Listening. It's so quiet that the only sound is the sigh of *Voilà*'s wake.

They hear, "South-southeast, sir. Two to three knots."

She's close! Did they hear an accent in that voice?

The wind itself holds its breath. Eamon cups his ears and scans from side to side. *Where are they?*

"No soundings, sir," comes from the other ship, and *Voilà*'s crew nearly jumps out of their skins. It sounds close enough that it could have come from their own deck! And it's answered. "Very well, lay off soundings."

What is this ship going to look like? How close can they pass without seeing each other?

"Hard to starboard!" Harper shouts down from the rigging with no attempt to whisper. Cook swings the wheel over fast, and *Voilà* rounds up toward the wind. A shadow looms ahead and grows large. Luckily, the other ship's helmsman has mistaken Harper's call for their own. In the arc of the two ships turning, Marco watches the other's bowsprit miss *Voilà*'s rigging by only yards. Her own goes from aiming at the mystery ship's bow to pointing past her stern. In fog, *Voilà*'s sails are wet and heavy. They luff lazily in the near calm. Harper stares through the fog up to the other ship's lookout, who gapes back at him. Aboard both boats, the sailors stand silently, their voices stuck in their throats. In slow motion and near silence, the two ships slide past each other portside to portside, almost within distance to jump from one to the other. The splash of their bow waves echo between the two hulls. The larger ship has boats stacked on deck and no gunports. As each helm passes by abreast of the other, a man stands at the rail of the larger ship looking down.

Bruno half raises his right hand, but before he can wave, the other ship's transom goes by. He reads her name on her stern as her American flag fades into the fog. Finding his voice, he bellows, "Ahoy, *Artemis*! From whence do you hail?"

"Ahoy! We're out of Nantucket this day, bound for the Pacific. What ship are you and where from?" Distance starts to fade the officer's voice.

"We are the *Voilà*, departed the Caribbean three and twenty days ago, bound for Marblehead."

"Fair winds!" are the last words they can shout to each other.

"Damn, that was close!" Bruno shakes his head. "A whaler, it was. Cook, come back to west by north."

"West by north it is," Cook answers.

Adrenaline has sharpened everyone. "Eamon, start soundings. When you find bottom, we'll come up to north."

"What's your plan?"

"We're south of Cape Cod, and no shallows reach out from there. So, we'll sail the ten-fathom curve along the shore. That will point us to Marblehead."

"That'll be a lee shore," Sophie points out.

"And a beam reach," Bruno answers. "We can bear up if need be."

As they sail the Cape's coast, the fog lifts. It's a moonless night, and bright stars feel like lost friends. They pass Provincetown shortly before dawn.

"Much as I'm glad to be out of the fog, we'll not sail past Boston in broad daylight," Bruno declares. "We'll heave to inside the Cape for the day and time our transit for after nightfall."

"Oh, Eamon," Sophie consoles, "it must unsettle you, only fifty miles from home and having to wait."

"True enough, I don't feel in my right mind, but it's not as if anyone expects me. It's taken so long; there's no such thing as late anymore."

Voilà rounds the tip of Cape Cod and sails another hour into the bay. There she rounds up into the wind until she loses all way. They leave the jibs aback, the foresail free, and the main close hauled. With her helm hard to starboard, she slowly drifts sideways to port.

"It should take eight or nine hours to reach Marblehead," Bruno estimates. "If we make way at dusk, it will be dark by the time Boston is abeam. Well and good if we slip by unseen, but if the blockade catches sight of us, we'll need to tack out. Rest up. It could be a long night."

As *Voilà* drifts, Eamon sits on the forward hatch, looks in the distance, and grows anxious.

Marco appears beside him. "How do you fare?"

"I don't know. Nervous, I suppose. And scared."

After Marco, it's Sophie who joins them. She brings Cook with her, and Harper leaves the helm and makes his excuse. "The helm's lashed to weather anyway. It looked like a meetin' up here. I'll get the captain and Smith."

They all ask him about his family. He waxes heartbreakingly and worries. "What if she's given up? What if she sold the shop and is not even there? And I've changed so much! What if we're all strangers now? Will the children be afraid of me? Will printing come back to me? Curse me! In her letter, Amy asked what I would bring back for her, and I don't have anything!" Each time he veers into his fears, the others divert him.

"No matter what you come home to," Cook endorses, "you made it. Your chances were slight to none, but you did it."

"You've been tested," Bruno adds, "beyond all hope. You've been tested, and you've rung true. Don't ever doubt yourself. You've done all you could."

"And Becca," Sophie chimes in, "she's been tested no less than you. No matter how, if she's there and the children are well, she's true, too. Even if you *are* strangers, you still love her. I know it in my bones, and so do you. Amy and Alex, too. I've heard it in your voice."

"What lies ahead of ya," Cook adds, "is unknown, but it always has been. You know them, and they know you in ways no one else can. Trust that and each other. Whatever's next, you'll bear it."

"For heaven's sake, it'll be grand," Marco insists. "It's your home!" A little while later, he brings a souvenir to Eamon. "This is called a chambered nautilus. I got it in Australia. It's a small one, but maybe Amy will like it."

"And here's a piece of my scrimshaw." Harper hands it to him. "That's a picture of *Voilà*. For Alex."

Sophie is next with one more thing. "This pendant is made of Connemara marble, from Ireland. All I've got for it is this string, I don't have a chain, but you should have something for Becca, too."

"It's beautiful. All of it. Thank you, all three." Eamon's throat is too tight for more words to escape. While harshness and uncaring have toughened him, it's in the face of kindness that he cannot hold tears back.

Cook walks up with a bucket of hot water, a cloth, and a bar of soap. "Thought you might want to shine yourself up."

"Do they know you with a beard?" Sophie asks. "I'm no good with a razor, but I can trim it for you, and you've seen me cutting everyone's hair."

Eamon nods and whispers, "Thank you."

❋ ❋ ❋

At dusk, Bruno calls, "Let's tack the headsails across and sheet home the fores'l. Cook, give us north-northwest."

"North-northwest it is."

Voilà picks up speed. The tension on board is palpable. They cross paths with a row of cumulus clouds, each dropping virga. The glow of dusk lights up these thin curtains of rain. Ghostly shapes appear in the sky in shades of pink, orange, and gold and then vanish. This goes on for an hour. *Voilà*'s crew drinks in the coming and going of these diaphanous beings until it is fully dark. That's when the distant loom of Boston's lights glows off the port bow.

By eleven o'clock, *Voilà* makes a peaceful four knots, and Boston is abeam fifteen miles distant. The lanterns of what must be a blockading ship are well off to port. *Voilà* shows no lights. Her decks quiet, her crew lost in thoughts, there seems to be nothing to blockade running. This is shattered when cannon fire erupts from the distant ship. They all duck, but there is no ascending whine of a cannonball's approach. An answering broadside shakes the sky around them again, the flash of cannon fire lighting the near distance toward the city. They want to run from these adversaries, intent upon each other's destruction. Run from death. There are screams and shouts amid musket fire and another volley of crash and boom. *Voilà* and crew concussed by the cannon fire, wary of errant arsenal, they wince and duck with each blast. Far enough off that they may slip by unseen, they beg of *Voilà* more speed and escape. The battle rages and falls astern. Echoes chase them until the fierceness fades to a conclusion they shudder to imagine.

At 4 a.m., the wind is light, and *Voilà* ghosts toward Gale's Head Fort at the mouth of Marblehead Harbor. To arouse no suspicion, Marco stands at the bow with a lantern lighting her headsails. Sophie shines another onto the French tricolor at her stern.

"Avast there!" comes the call from shore. "What ship are you?"

"We are the schooner *Voilà*," Bruno shouts back, "merchant from Isle de France, here from the Indies to trade."

"Stand by."

"Very well," he returns, and then to Cook at the helm he says, "round up."

Cook turns her into the wind. From the fort, the soldiers hear no orders from *Voilà*'s deck, yet the sails, one by one, appear to evaporate into the dark as they are struck. The main and one jib still fly. Head to wind, she starts to drift aft when an officer calls, "Proceed to anchor and remain on board. The harbormaster will expect your captain in the morning."

"Aye-aye, sir, and thank you."

The eastern sky starts to lighten by the time they anchor and square *Voilà* away. Going below, fresh aromas from the galley welcome them. After they all shed a layer of clothing, Bruno raises his hot mug to toast, "Well done, mates, and welcome home, Eamon."

"Here, here!" the rest of the crew cheers.

CHAPTER 32

BRUNO ROWED THE skiff to shore. He said I can take it after he clears with the harbormaster. Cook and Sophie want to come with me. They all do, except Smith. Somehow, their caring pains me, but I'll go alone. Once I'm on the pier, I could walk blindfolded. I'll knock on my own door. . . . Is it mine? Is she there? And Alex and Amy. They'll be in school.

When will Bruno return? Not soon enough yet too soon. Lord, I'm scared and have been for too long. I hate being scared. I can't sit still, so I pace the deck. Thank you, Voilá. Sophie is right. You are a little world and a better one. But you're no longer my home.

It's a lucky thing we sailed all night. I wouldn't have been able to sleep. First that near collision and then when those cannons went off, my heart nearly stopped. Dying so close to home would have been cruel indeed. How can they kill each other? How do they face it and not run? Me? It's this day I face. My battle has been long, but I've made it. 'Tis over now. I can lay myself down. This warming scene is home at last.

✸ ✸ ✸

"Very well." The harbormaster signs an official looking paper and hands it back to Bruno. "You're all clear. In this embargo, your cargo will be welcome. Have a good day."

Bruno folds the paper into his logbook but doesn't exit, clears his throat, and asks, "Is there a family here name of McGrath?"

The response he sees is shock. Is there something else besides? "Why do you ask? Have you got a post from Eamon? Or news?"

Bruno hesitates. Maybe he's already gone too far. He's listed six crew but hasn't had to name them.

The harbormaster fills the silence. "Have you met him? You must've met him. Or . . ." He doesn't want bad news. "Where? When?"

This could get out of hand, Bruno thinks. "Yes, we met him in Isle de France. Ten or twelve months ago. He was well."

The man looks down and lets out a held breath. "Mercy. You should tell his family. Here, I'll draw you a map to the print shop, where they live. Upstairs."

Bruno folds this page into his logbook and rows back to *Voilá*.

❋ ❋ ❋

"We're free to roam." Bruno looks to me. "Anyone goin' ashore?"

"Eamon, don't forget this." Sophie hands me a canvas bag with my gifts in it. "You can get the rest of your things later. Are those your best clothes?" She stops herself. "Of course, they are. You'll bring your family aboard, will you not? And invite us to your home, certainly."

"Of course."

"We're good for a party," Cook chimes in.

My shipmates wish me well and luck. We all shake hands.

"Don't worry about the skiff," Bruno tells me. "We'll be ashore and pick it up when we want it."

"Don't be a stranger," Cook adds. "We'll check with the harbormaster for any word from you."

I climb down to the skiff and drop my bag in its bow. It wobbles with my weight until I turn around and sit on the thwart. Harper tosses its painter in and nods. I push off of *Voilá*'s hull and stroke toward State Street pier.

"Thank you," I call. "We'll see each other soon." They wave.

I feel my arms and shoulders pull on the oars, watching the swirl of water around their blades. The starboard oarlock squeaks with each pull. The vessels anchored in the harbor are animated by the ripple they float upon. They look like a flock of one-winged birds with their feathers tucked close, waiting to fly. Their bows all point in unison into the breeze. Rowing feels good. Between strokes, I check over my shoulder. *Still on course.* Stroke again. *Not hard, no hurry now.* Stroke. *I've made it.* Stroke. *I'm here.* Stroke.

The tide is out. The ramp from the pier down to the dock is steep. A covey of small rowboats nests together there. I ship my oars to coast toward them and grab the gunwale of the nearest, drape my bag over my head and across my chest, grab the painter, and step into the boat I've caught. They all sway and jiggle at my barging across. Crawling out of the last one and onto the dock's rough planks, I add my line to a cleat already buried in lines.

When I stand, I'm a little shaky. *Breathe, Eamon.* I turn for the ramp, grab its rail, and walk up. At the top, I stop and stare. *Marblehead! I know these people.* A nod here and smile there. I want to run to my shop and home but can't. I'm dizzy. *Can I even walk?*

❀ ❀ ❀

"Well, come on!" Sophie urges as soon as Eamon is lost from sight. "Get the gig in the water. Not on that side. He'll see it on that side."

"Calm down, woman," Bruno answers. "Stop your worrying. We'll get there. I have a map."

When the five of them are ready to shove off, Cook is at the helm while the other four will row.

"You're sure, Smith?" Sophie offers, "I mean, James. She'll not need a watch this morning."

"No, no. Go on. I can't leave her. Tell me about it when you get back."

They push away. At the pier, they nestle between the rest of the dinghies and help each other onto the dock. Cook huffs and puffs to the top of the ramp. Bruno pulls the page from his pocket. "This way." They bustle off, saying "Good morning" here and "Excuse me" there. The feel of a new place, new people, new air itself is fresh and exciting! It's a glorious morning.

❋ ❋ ❋

Tucker's wharf looks busy. Gilbert and Sons are building another fish boat. Tom Merrit stands on the steps of his Feed and Seed Store. And here's Jordan's fish market. Up the street is Beth Abbott's boarding house. Passing it, my mouth waters for her cooking. *Has the baker remarried?* All of it familiar, as if I never left, but it seems so long ago. It's a secret that I know them. Even if someone recognized me, I'm no longer who they knew. They can't know what I've seen and where I've been. I feel invisible, a ghost passing through. Disguised, but strangers don't go unnoticed here. *How many eyes have tripped over me?* If I detour, I'll pass the library and Town Hall. *Is Jim Crocker still mayor?* Doubling back, I stop and stare across the street. The shingle over the door is there: Books & Printing. So, it's time. Someone will get curious if I don't move. *This is it.* There's the open sign in the window, but I knock. Twice. I am trembling.

❋ ❋ ❋

At the other end of the block, Sophie peeks around the corner of a building. She sees Eamon crossing the street toward a house with a sign above its white door: Books & Printing. The door fronts onto the sidewalk. There is no yard.

"Did he already go in?" Marco worries.

"No, look. There he goes!" she reports.

Bruno, Cook, Harper, and Marco nearly push her out into the street to look around the corner too.

✻ ✻ ✻

Rebecca opens the door. "Good morn. We're open. How may I help you?"

She reaches inside the apron I used to wear to wipe her hands. Its front is black with ink. I wipe one eye and stand there.

"Are you hale, sir?"

God, oh my God! I blink back tears. I'm holding my breath.

"Sir?"

"Becca," I manage, "it's me."

There's a sudden and enormous conflict inside her. As if it will tear her open to get out. *Can her eyes grow any wider?*

She gasps. Her exhale is forced. Gasp. Anguish aloud. Gasp! I can't move, can't take my eyes off hers. A serrated cry escapes her. "Eamon?" Gasp! "You're alive!"

Her body collides with mine. I almost fall backward. My arms hug her too tightly; her arms squeeze the breath out of me. We are a human vise, but who needs to breathe? My eyes are shut tight.

I hear my voice. Saying something over and over. *What is it?* "I will never let you go, never let you go." There are people gathering on the sidewalk. *Who are they? Who cares?* "Never let you go. I love you so much."

She cries. Hysteric. *Or is it me?* There are words in her sobs. At last, I hear them buried into my shoulder. "But I let you go. You were dead, and I let you go."

Zachary Silvers stands in the doorway of the shop. He holds onto the doorjamb as though the ground quakes. *What is it that shakes him?*

✻ ✻ ✻

Sophie ducks away from the corner where she has been watching, slams her back into the wall behind her, and shakes her head. "Cac!"

"What?" Marco pleads.

"Don't you see?" She hisses back. "You can't see?" She meets the confused stare of these men, shakes her head, and drops her voice. "She's pregnant."

CHAPTER 33

ZACH LOOKS DOWN the street, anywhere but at us. "I'll get the children," he says.

"Thank you. Yes, please," Becca answers as we pull apart to arm's length, her studying my face, me trying to read her eyes. Releasing each other feels like a test of weak knees. We wipe our eyes. "Come in," she bids me, "please." The shop feels as I remember it, but I look only at her. She motions me to a chair, adding, "I must sit." We are speechless. How long, I don't know. Time stands still. What can we say?

Amy runs through the door. I hardly have time to stand before I catch her. Hugging her, I feel her in my bones, as if a piece of me was missing and has come back. I feel my pulse inside of her. Alex comes in. I reach for him, but he hesitates. *They are both so tall. The shirt he wears. Was it mine? Its cuffs rolled up?*

"I told everyone you'd come back," Amy declares.

Alex studies my face, bearded and leathered by the sun, as if I am a stranger. "Is it you? Really you?"

"Yes, 'tis I." I pull him into our embrace.

"What happened to your nose?"

"I broke it." I shrug. "Your voice is lower."

"You were gone so long," he says.

"Forgive me, please. I tried to get back as soon as I could, and I wrote to you from every port."

"But we received only the one letter."

"Only one?"

"When we heard no more," Becca tells from where she sits, "we thought you were dead."

"Only one. Damn!" I look down and back up. "I know I've changed, but it's me. It's me and I love you all so much. I didn't know how much. Not until I was taken and until now." I wipe tears from my face and reach for my bag, grateful for a distraction. "Here. I have something for each of you."

Zach stands at the doorway again. I want to throw him out. To be alone with my family. Do I owe him thanks for helping them? We only nod to each other, and he leaves.

✳ ✳ ✳

Later this day, I sit at Maggie's table. Her children are here. Elizabeth sits beside her, wrapped by her mother's arm. Maggie leans back against Ben, whose Eleanor stands with him. He appears rooted and holds his mother's shoulders. Timothy stands close by. Jacob, too, though he feels aloof, to us and to himself. I don't remember reaching across the table for Maggie's hand. Rebecca, Alex, and Amy stand at my back.

"It grieves me to bring sad news to you," I start. I tell them about Sam's doctoring. About his costume as one of Neptune's mermaids. How much he missed them and land itself. "He was coming back to you." I tell them how he saved *Atalanta* and all the lives aboard her. Maggie's many tears are silent. She manages an admiring comment of Sam to prompt a smile from us, a split second's relief. Throughout our conversation, one of us sniffs. I describe the view from where he is buried. I tell them about the sunset at our last visit to his grave. When the color in the sky lit the sea afire and Coop wondered if it was Sam's spirit saying goodbye.

"I gave up," Maggie tells us. "Some time ago, I let go of him, though I didn't say it. Lord help me, I'm giving him up again. Out loud this time."

We are all silent, each within him or herself. Wanting to comfort each other, we look up and breathe again. In these few minutes, Maggie and I are already old friends. She insists upon meeting my shipmates and feeding everyone. Marshaling us, she is as good as any captain. The women head for their kitchens; the men go to market. I tell her I must stop by the cooper's.

"Of course." She nods. "Invite them as well."

Amy clings to me. Alex steps aside, but does he want to? Having witnessed Maggie, it jolts me to imagine the scars they bear. I ask them to come with me.

I tell Coop's parents how their son thrives. How he rises to every challenge like he was made for it. He could sign on to any ship as carpenter. I tell them about his tattoos and to not be surprised when their son sails into Marblehead as the captain of a mighty ship.

It is a *most* awkward evening. One that Zachary Silvers does not attend. Conversation is hesitant. I eat little. There is a palpable confusion. *Do we celebrate, or do we grieve? Can both happen at the same time?*

The strangest thing is to row back to *Voilá*. I hadn't imagined it: Becca wrapping her arms around Amy to keep her from coming after me, stopping me, trying to find some way for me to sleep at home. *Home?* I wonder. Me promising that I will be back at dawn. Amy's crying eyes piercing me.

Cook breaks out the rum, and I welcome its numbing. Bruno encourages me to stay on as crew, but I cannot think to leave. I've barely arrived. No matter how much I have changed, I belong here with my family. *My family? Yes, my family!* Cook compliments the meal, Harper the tobacco. I assure Smith that he will have his documents and tell Marco he can have any book he wants from our shop. *Our shop?*

After the previous night underway, I am exhausted but cannot lay myself down. At last, sleep takes me while I sit at the table.

The children all want to see *Voilá*, so we row them out to her the next day. They return to shore excited and convince the adults to come too. Cook invites everyone to feast aboard *Voilá* before she sails. After she sails, I lodge at Beth's boarding house.

To speak privately, Rebecca and I step out for a walk each day. We keep to quieter streets and parks. We nod to people's attentions. A brave few shake my hand. "We've heard of your return," they say. "Welcome home."

"Thank you." We keep walking and stop a little further on.

"Eamon," she says, "you and Zach and I need to talk."

My heart freezes. "Of course, but let us at least wait until the children are in school and we can be alone."

The next Monday, they close the shop. She suggests we sit at the table upstairs.

"No," I answer. "It no longer feels like my home. I cannot be comfortable there."

So, we sit upon two stools and a chair amid the desk, the press, and racks of type. We are surrounded by shelves of paper, books, small casks of ink, and countless tools. The storefront windows let in shaded morning light. I had forgotten the aromas of ink and paper, wood and leather.

In Zach's eyes, I see pain, fear, and confusion. Not defiance, nor pride. Before this, I wanted to hurt him, but now his humility disarms me.

"I don't belong here," Zach starts. "You two married years ago. With you now back from the dead, you are still married. I . . . I should leave."

"Zach, wait." Rebecca puts her hand on his shoulder. "Please, don't presume anything. You cannot belong anywhere else when this is our baby." She cradles her belly.

"I never meant to have feelings for another man's wife," he continues. "If I had known you were alive, Eamon, this would not have happened. I only meant to help."

"And we needed his help," Becca adds. "With you gone, we needed everyone's help. Without it, what would have become of us?"

"I know," I manage to say.

"The harbormaster told us no one returns from being shanghaied, and when we heard no more from you . . ."

"Becca, please," I ask, and she stops.

For a moment, we hold silence between us.

"Zach, I would thank you, but I can't," I say quietly. "Not yet. For two and a half years, all that kept me alive was my love for my family and wanting to return to them, but now I am here, and I face more betrayal." My voice builds. I start to shake. "I am angry and cannot forgive that my wife is your wife. That you and she share our bed. Damnit, I could break your neck! My hands are strong enough, but I am tired of being strong and tired of anger, and what would breaking your neck change?"

"But we have not betrayed you." Becca cries openly. "This is the same betrayal that started when you were taken, and we have *all* suffered it. I waited as long as I could for you, Eamon, and for another letter from you. When it did not come, like Maggie, I gave up, and it hurt! I, too, could not cry it aloud!"

"Good!" I am shocked by my reply. "I am gladdened that it hurt, that you know the pain I felt and feel now." When I can speak again, I confess, "I am sorry. I don't mean that. It shames me that I said it."

"No, Eamon, do not apologize," she grants. "But do not ask me to be sorry. We are innocent, and so are you."

"Are we?" I feel myself tremble. "I do not know what you've lived through, and you know even less of what has changed me, but I do not feel innocent. Because you thought me dead, you may be innocent, but I never thought you were dead." I am tongue-tied until I meet Becca's questioning eyes. "I never thought you were dead, yet I had my pleasures with another woman."

Before I can explain, she does not hesitate. "Then I forgive *you*."

"I went back to her as often as I could . . ."

"Stop!" she shouts. "Have we not suffered enough?"

I shake my head. My cheeks are wet. "What a sorrowful lot ours is."

"Is it?" she asks. "Is it sorrowful that you are not dead? Is it sad that Zach and I will soon cherish a newborn babe? This is bigger than us, Eamon. And I'll not ever apologize for loving either of you."

"How can you love us both?" I ask.

"The same way that when Amy was born, I loved Alex no less. You know this. As their father, you love them as much as I do. And I'll love this next child as well." She rubs her belly. "Love is not a quantity, Eamon, it's a quality. My heart can hold us all, and so can yours. Despite what the rest of Marblehead may think, you are good men, and I am a good woman!"

"Pray, what of that?" I beg for an answer. "We do not care to share you as wife, and the church will not allow you two husbands. In fact, it will condemn our family."

"That's why I am the one who should leave," Zach says.

"I am not yours to divvy between you!" She is angry. "And I'll hear no more of sorrow."

"All this time," I tell them, "I believed with my whole being that I belonged here, but now that I am back, I cannot pick up where I left off, and I cannot start over."

"Eamon," Zach says, "of course you belong here. I've done my best for your family, but I am not Alex and Amy's father. Your children love and need you. I cannot come between you and them."

"Please know," Becca says to me, "they will always love you, and so will I. However you have changed, I still know you, and you know me."

I look back to her. "Yes, we were all betrayed. I thought that it would end if I returned, but it doesn't end, and we cannot pretend it did not happen."

"Then we will learn to live with it," she says this with such force that it rings true.

※ ※ ※

Witnessing my children scores me deepest. When I vanished from them, he was twelve and she was eight, but we've lost something more than time. We've lost trust. I see it in their eyes, feel it in Alex's hesitation. After what befell us, how can we trust anything? And without trust, will we ever laugh again?

"The day I was taken from you, I died. Truly, I felt life leave me, but it didn't leave, or it came back. To be alive and here with you is a miracle. Even before I was taken, it always was. I did not realize that, not until I was gone. I'd not wish what happened to us on anyone, yet I hold some of it dear. Of those moments, if you had seen them, you would understand of what I speak, but what I lived through is more than I can tell."

Alex asks about the life of a sailor. Amy listens to my stories, asks for more, and, unknown to us, writes them down.

EPILOGUE

THE QUESTION REBECCA wrote to me has become my own: how do I do this?

How do I come back to a life that has gone on without me and when I am no longer who I was? Miraculous to make it home, yet painful to be here, how do I do this?

Becca harbors no such uncertainty, though, and to protect her and the innocent babe, to legitimize their marriage, she and I annul ours. I *have* changed, and this fits the restlessness I feel when I have nowhere to go and when domestic life asks more of me. When *Voilá* drifted in Cape Cod Bay, I feared what I would return to. I did not realize that I feared leaving the sea, feared that the sky would lose its importance, that the horizon would become irrelevant.

After giving birth, Becca is no help in "our" print shop. This forces Zach and me to work together. Our tempers are quick to flare, but our fatherhood must rise to meet her motherhood. Two years on, my help is more trying than useful. Lodging at Beth's boarding house, I meet sailors who are between sailings, and I start to look for a small ship to crew or captain. On coastal trade, I could return home often.

Alex wants to go to sea and could crew for me, but he wants to circle the globe. His dreams are answered when he and I are sailing our little dory around the harbor and *Voilá* sails in. I thought I would never see her again, but with the war over and no blockade to run, here she is. Our enthusiasm overflows to hail each other. When they promise to bring Alex back, we all let go of him.

Finally, Coop's widowed father proudly shows me a letter from his son. Coop is the second mate of a clipper sailing in Asia's tea trade.

Looking back, how did I get here? I recall Mister Ames's offer and his wondering if my life was waiting for me. I feel Sam's longing to belong somewhere, anywhere, home. But why does Jack come to mind, his gambler's luck, the purses he held and the coins he flipped? Without two sides, there *is* no "coin" to flip. Is it essential to meet beauty *and* grief? Are we meant to laugh and weep? To be anything, must life include everything?

".. . Admit that once you have got up
from your chair and opened the door,
once you have walked out into the clean air
toward that edge and taken the path up high
beyond the ordinary, you have become
the privileged and the pilgrim,
the one who will tell the story
and the one, coming back
from the mountain,
who helped to make it."

MAMEEN by David Whyte

Cast of characters:

Eamon McGrath (pronounced Aim-en') (36 years old), Sam Holbrook (40), Coop (16), Jack (50)

Atalanta: three masted full-rigged ship 170'LOD, 220'LOA, 35'beam, 18'draft, 140'height, 700 tons

Captain Rolinson (50), first/chief mate Duncan (39), second mate Strom (28), bosun Gates

Crew: Swede, Spanky, Chips, Cook, Axel, Johnny, Toren

First mate toughs: Will'm, Paddy, Rye

McGrath family—Rebecca (33), Amanda (8), Alex (12).

Holbrook family—Maggie (40), Ben (18), Timothy (15), Jacob (13), Elizabeth (11); Ben's girlfriend—Eleanor Smith

Recruits: Felipe, Vasco, and unnamed

Pualani—Sam's girlfriend in Hawaii

Zachary Silvers—helps at the print shop (thirty)

Ship owners—Ames, Cohen, Levi

Consorts—Mingzhu, Tu

Chinese recruits—Tommy, Hiro, Yao

African recruit—Moses

From Mauritius—Andre, Stephen

Mauritius—governor Robert Farquhar, Captain Parker, Commodore Rowley

Voilà: gaff rig topsail schooner, 75'LOD, 95 LOA, 60'LWL, 19'beam, 12'draft, 80'height, 70tons

Voilà—Captain Bruno (38), Sophie (28), Marco (23), Cook (56), Harper (40), Smith (30)

Glossary

Aback—wind filling the "back" side of a sail

Abaft or aft—toward the stern

Abeam—directly off the side of a ship

Aft deck—the deck at the stern, aft of the aft mast

Aloft—up in the rigging, on masts and yardarms

Astern—behind a ship

Atalanta—a Greek goddess of the hunt, raised by a bear, known to be very fast

Baggy wrinkle—chafing gear made of old rope, looks like a bushy tail attached to rigging

Batten—a thin wood slat that fits in a sleeve sewn in a sail, to stiffen the sail's shape

Beam—the middle and widest dimension of a boat or ship

Bells—system for keeping time on a ship in four-hour segments, ringing a bell every half hour.

Below—below the decks, inside the ship

Belaying pin—iron or wooden peg fitted into railing to secure lines

Bilge—inside a ship where the hull meets the keel, at the very bottom, where water collects

Binnacle—the structure that supports the steering wheel and compass

Block and tackle—a block is a pulley; the rope between two pulleys is a tackle

Bone in her teeth—the white wave and the bow of a ship sailing fast

Boom—the spar at the bottom of a fore-and-aft-rigged (not square-rigged) sail

Bosun—(short for boatswain) in charge of rigging and calling crew to duty

Bow—the front end of a boat or ship (opposite of stern)

Bowsprit—beam that protrudes over the water from the bow of a ship

Brace—line used to control horizontal movement of yardarms

Broach—when a ship turns sideways to wind and waves and rolls far over to one side

Bulwark—waist-high wall and railing that surrounds a deck

Bulkhead—below deck partition or wall

Buntlines—lines used to haul up the body of a square sail to its yard

Careen—to intentionally beach a ship at high tide for the purpose of cleaning and scraping its bottom during low tide and float her again at high tide

Cat-o'-nine-tails—a short whip with nine sharp strands that extend a few feet beyond its handle. It was stored in a leather bag between uses. The term "cat's out of the bag" traces to when a man was going to be beaten.

Cathead—beam protruding from the side of the bow that suspends the anchor over the water

Chain plates—massive metal hardware on the hull sides that shrouds attach to

Cleat—piece of hardware around which ropes/lines are tied

Clipper—three or four masted ship, square-rigged

Coming about—tacking upwind, the bow passing through the wind direction

Companionway—a doorway and steps between above and below decks

Compass rose—circle showing the compass as a star pattern of four points (north, east, south, and west) or eight points (adding NE, SE, SW, NW) sixteen points (i.e., SSW), thirty-two points (i.e., north by east . . .)

Cooper—a maker of barrels

Course—lowest and biggest of the square sails; also the direction a
ship sails

Crosstrees—wood structure that joins upper and lower masts and
spreads shrouds for support

Davits—a pair of curved posts with a pulley at their ends that can
pivot to hang over the water to raise and lower a ship's dinghy,
skiff, or longboat

Davy Jones—fiend who presides over the evil spirits of the deep, lives
at the bottom of the sea

Deadeye—a wooden block through which lines are led to connect
rigging

Dirty weather—stormy

Displacement—the weight of a ship

Doldrums—areas of little wind on either side of the equator

Downwind—toward the direction *toward* which the wind blows

Draft—water depth required to float a vessel

Earring—short lines in the middle of a sail to tie reefed sail cloth to
the boom, yardarm, or itself

Eight bells—12:00, 4:00, or 8:00 and the change of the watch

Fathom—six feet

First mate—or mate, or chief mate, second-in-command

Five bells—2:30, 6:30, or 10:30

Flemish horse—a short and separate footrope at the ends of the
yardarms

Fo'csle—short for Forecastle, the crew's cabin at the bow of a ship

Foot—the bottom edge of a sail

Footrope—rope beneath a yardarm for the sailors to stand on while
    furling, reefing, setting sails

Fore and aft rigged—sail attached vertically at its forward edge to a
    stay or mast

Foredeck—the deck at the bow, forward of the foremast

Foremast—the forward mast

Forward—toward the bow of a boat or ship

Four bells—2:00, 6:00, or 10:00

Fresh weather—windy, stormy weather (opposite of light weather)

Gig—(or wherry) a fast boat for rowing or sailing ashore (stowed on
    a ship's deck)

Gimballed—balanced on rings and pivots to stay level while a ship
    pitches, tips, and heels

Glass—telescope

Gooseneck—connection that secures a boom to a mast

Grog—a drink of rum and water

Gudgeons—the fittings at the aft edge of the keel, from which the
    rudder is suspended

Gunwale or gunnel—the edge of a boat or ship (and its railing/
    bulwark)

Hailing port—where a ship is from, written below her name on the
    transom

Halyard—line used to raise sails or yardarms

Hard tack—a very basic dried biscuit

Hawser—a thick line or cable between a ship and an anchor or dock

Head to wind—steering straight into the wind

Heave to—turning the course upwind with the sails aback to stop
    the ship

Heeling—when a ship's sails are full, she tips or leans to the leeward
    side

Helm—noun: binnacle and steering wheel; verb: to steer the ship

Helmsman—the person steering a ship

Hike out—to lean over the edge of a small sailboat on the side

opposite the sail to balance weight against the force in the sail
and level the boat

Hold—space below decks for cargo

The Horn—Cape Horn (at the south end of South America)

Jack tar—nickname or slang for an experienced sailor (also "salty
dog")

Jib—a staysail between the foremast and the bowsprit or foredeck

Jibe—to tack downwind, the stern passing through the wind direction

Knighthead—vertical timbers on deck on either side of the bowsprit

Larboard—dated term for the portside of a ship

Lead line—a weight on the end of a long string to measure the depth

League—approximately 2.5 nautical miles

Lee shore—a shore to leeward (downwind) of a boat

Leeward—the side of the ship opposite the windward side, the lower
side when heeling

Lines—ropes, or the look of a ship ("nice lines" = pretty and likely
fast)

Listing—tipping to either side when in calm water and wind, not
level

LOA—length overall (including bowsprit)

LOD—length on deck (excluding bowsprit)

Longboat—a larger rowing/sailing boat for going ashore and
exploring

LWL—length at the waterline

Luff—noun: the forward or leading edge of a fore-and-aft-rigged sail;
verb: when a sail flaps (like a flag)

Make way—to keep moving through the water (enough to maintain
steerage)

Make fast—to tie in place

Mainmast—the middle and tallest mast

Marlinspike seamanship—the parceling, serving, whipping of lines
(includes decorative patterns of string and twine)

Man of war—a navy ship made for war (equipped with cannons and soldiers)

Mast—vertical wooden spar to support rigging, yardarms, and sails

Masthead—the top of a mast

Mizzen—the aft mast

Nautical mile—1.15 statute miles

Noon sight—use of a sextant when the sun passes highest overhead, to approximate longitude

Off her lines—a ship listing or deeper in bow or stern

Oil skins—raincoats and rain pants made of oiled canvas

On her lines—a ship sitting level in the water, not listing to either side nor deeper in bow or stern

One bell—12:30, 4:30, or 8:30

Overhead—ceiling

Painter—the bow line of a small boat

Parceling—wrapping canvas strips tightly around a rope

Pintles—the pins at the forward edge of the rudder, fit into the gudgeons, and act like a hinge

Points of a compass—the circle of a compass divided into 32 "points" recited by name instead of number (i.e., 090 = east), like northeast, east by north, south-southwest, etc . . .

Port—looking from the stern to the bow, the left side of a ship

Quarter—the aft corner of a ship forward of the stern and aft of the beam

Quarterdeck—a ship's upper deck at the stern

Rail—see *gunwale*

Ratlines—horizontal ropes lashed between the shrouds, as a rope ladder

Rhumb line—the shortest distance from a ship to its destination

Rigging—all the lines, ropes, masts, and spars that hoist, trim, and hold masts and sails aloft

Rode—the rope and/or chain that connects a ship to its anchor

Round up—to turn the ship so it heads straight into the wind

Royal—square-rigged sail, high up, above the topgallant and below the skysail

Running rigging—the lines and ropes that can be pulled in and let out

"Sail ho"—says that a sailing vessel has been sighted

Scrimshaw—illustration carved/scored into a whale tooth

Scupper—hole in the gunwale and bulwark to let water drain off the deck

Second mate—third in command

Sea legs—being steady in stride and stance despite a ship's motion

Serving—binding twine around a rope to keep it from chafing

Set and struck—to hoist a sail and take it back down

Seven bells—3:30, 7:30, or 11:30

Sheet—line used to pull a fore and aft rigged sail in or let it out, to trim it

Shipway—a slope on which a ship is build and down which it slides when launched

Shot of chain—ninety feet

Shrouds—ropes or cables side to side that keep the masts from falling down

Six bells—3:00, 7:00, or 11:00

Skiff—a small row or sail boat

Skysail—the highest of the square-rigged sails (except sometimes topped by a moonsail)

Slew—to turn or slide uncontrollably in a direction

Sole—floor or deck

Son of a gun—in harbor, if a woman visited a man on board a warship, they might find privacy on the gun deck. Infers a natural born sailor was conceived there (by a gun).

Spanker—lowest sail fore and aft rigged on mizzenmast, usually gaff-rigged

Spar—general term for masts, yards, booms, gaffs, sprits, etc . . . made of wood

Sprit—short for bowsprit

Square-rigged—a sail attached/set horizontally from a yardarm

Standing rigging—stays and shrouds, not regularly trimmed, they keep the masts standing

Starboard—looking from the stern to the bow, the right-hand side of a ship

Stays—ropes or cables fore and aft that keep the masts from falling down

Stays'l or staysail—fore and aft rigged sail with its luff attached to a stay (not a mast)

Stern—the back of a boat or ship (opposite of bow)

Stoning—scrubbing the decks clean with a pumice like stone

Stuns'ls or studding sails—extra sails hoisted to extend beyond the ends of the yardarms

Sweat—to sweat a line, one end is attached to what is being pulled; the other end is attached to a cleat or belaying pin; the person sweating the line pulls on the middle of the line between these two attachments, and a person at the cleat or pin takes up any slack as the first person lets go of the line (called sweating because as the strands of the line squeeze tighter, water in them drips off like sweat)

Tacking—changing course so the wind that was blowing over one side now blows over the other

Taffrail—the upper part of the railing at the stern of a ship

Taffrail log—instrument towed astern that spins a meter to measure distance traveled

Tarring—painting a tar-like preservative on standing rigging

Tholepins—short vertical pieces of wood, in pairs, along the edge of a rowboat to hold an oar, placed between them, in place while rowing

Three bells—1:30, 5:30, or 9:30

Topgallant—square-rigged sail above the topsails and below the royal

Topsails—upper and lower, squared-rigged sail above the courses

Trade winds—continual east to west winds, located north and south of the doldrums

Transom—the surface that is the stern of a boat or ship

Turks head—decorative knot

Two bells—1:00, 5:00, or 9:00

Upwind—toward the direction *from* which the wind blows

Watch schedule—middle watch: midnight to 4am

    morning watch: 4am to 8am

    forenoon watch: 8am to noon

    afternoon watch: noon to 4pm

    1st dog watch: 4pm to 6pm (the off watch eats supper)

    2st dog watch: 6pm to 8pm (the off watch eats supper)

    8pm to midnight: first watch

Weather gauge—area upwind or to windward (or "to weather") of another ship

"Way-on"—motion through water (headway is moving forward; sternway is moving aft; underway is not anchored or docked, can mean adrift)

Weigh anchor—to lift the anchor to get underway

"Well down"—describes something beyond the horizon such that only the top of it is visible

"Where away"—asks where the object is sighted relative to this ship's anatomy

Windward—the side of the ship that the wind is blowing over, the higher side when heeling

Yankee—a big jib (to catch more wind when the winds are light)

Yard—short for yardarm—horizontal beam on a mast from which square sails hang

Acknowledgments

I THANK MY brother Marc for long ago sharing his desire to write, my sister Ann for her edits, and my family for being articulate. Thank you, friends Mary Roy, Jim Lawrence, Shaun Hubbard, Jane Wentworth, and Greg Byrne, for braving rough drafts and giving feedback. To friends who, over years, encouraged my writing, thank you Amy Wells, Erin Halcomb, Heather Roberts, Steve Krischel and more not listed here but not forgotten. Thank you, square-rigger Drew Hyslop, for applying your expertise to what I guessed (I've yet to sail on a square-rigged ship. . . . Anyone out there need crew?). Thank you, my friend and (as good luck would have it) publicist, Alice Acheson. Publishing's waters were uncharted for me. Without your help, this book would have run aground. I owe thanks to my publisher, Koehler Books. David Whyte, your poetry grew more important for me while I was offshore. Thank you for permitting me to bookend *Shanghaied* with excerpts from "SELF-PORTRAIT" and "MAMEEN." And Liza Michaelson, my beloved, thank you for believing in this story and my need to finish writing it. Your listening and many suggestions and edits made *Shanghaied* a better book. Finally, I am grateful for the horizons, metaphors, and lessons that sailing reveals.